GATEWAY TO THE UNIVERSE

CRAIG MARTELLE   JUSTIN SLOAN   MICHAEL ANDERLE

This book is a work of fiction. All of the characters, organizations, and events portrayed in this novel are either products of the author's imagination or are used fictitiously. Sometimes both.

Copyright © 2021 Craig Martelle, Justin Sloan and Michael Anderle
Cover by Andrew Dobell, www.creativeedgestudios.co.uk
Cover copyright © LMBPN Publishing

LMBPN Publishing supports the right to free expression and the value of copyright. The purpose of copyright is to encourage writers and artists to produce the creative works that enrich our culture.

The distribution of this book without permission is a theft of the author's intellectual property. If you would like permission to use material from the book (other than for review purposes), please contact support@lmbpn.com. Thank you for your support of the author's rights.

LMBPN Publishing
PMB 196, 2540 South Maryland Pkwy
Las Vegas, NV 89109

First US edition, October 2017
Version 1.06 March 2021

The Kurtherian Gambit (and what happens within / characters / situations / worlds) are copyright © 2015-2021 by Michael T. Anderle.

❀ Created with Vellum

CHARACTERS & TIMELINE

World's Worst Day Ever (WWDE)

WWDE + 20 years, Terry Henry returns from self-imposed exile. The Terry Henry Walton Chronicles detail his adventures from that time to WWDE+150

WWDE + 150 years – Michael returns to earth. BA returns to earth. TH & Char go to Space

Key Players

Terry Henry Walton (was 45 on the WWDE) – called TH by his friends, Enhanced with nanocytes by Bethany Anne herself (now Empress of the Federation), wears the rank of Colonel, leads the Force de Guerre (FDG), a military unit that he established on WWDE+20

Charumati (was 65 on the WWDE) – A Werewolf, married to Terry, carries the rank of Major in the FDG

Kimber (born WWDE+15, adopted approximately WWDE+25 by TH & Char, enhanced on WWDE+65) – Major in the FDG

- Her husband **Auburn Weathers** (enhanced on

WWDE+82) – provides logistics support to the FDG

- Their son, **Kailin** (enhanced on WWDE+93)

Kaeden (born WWDE+16, adopted approximately WWDE+24 by TH & Char, enhanced on WWDE+65) – Major in the FDG

- His wife **Marcie Spires** (born on WWDE+22, naturally enhanced) – Colonel in the FDG
- Their children Mary Ellen & William, born WWDE+60/61, did not get enhanced

Cory (born WWDE+25, naturally enhanced, gifted with the power to heal)

- Her husband **Ramses** (born WWDE+23, enhanced on WWDE+65) – Major in the FDG
- Their children Sarah (born WWDE+126, naturally enhanced) and Sylvia (born WWDE+127, naturally enhanced)

Vampires

- Valerie (born WWDE+108, transformed into a vampire at WWDE+140) – Transformed by the Duke, along with brother Donovan outside of Old Paris. She left to go to America and intercept/stop her brother's invasion of the land in his attempt to spread the domain of him and

his Foresaken. Became a daywalker after Michael himself gave her his blood.
- Robin (born WWDE+132, transformed into a vampire at WWDE+149) – Rescued by Valerie when she was in assassin training with a group called the Black Plague.

<u>**Werewolves**</u> born before the WWDE:

- Sue & Timmons
- Shonna & Merrit
- Ted (with Felicity, an enhanced human)

<u>**Weretigers**</u> born before the WWDE:

- Aaron & Yanmei

<u>**Forsaken**</u>

- Joseph (born 300 years before the WWDE)
- Petricia (born WWDE+30)

<u>**Unenhanced Humans**</u>

- Tyson Kurtz, Lieutenant in the Force de Guerre
- Garcia, Sergeant in the FDG
- Samantha Matthews, Private in the FDG
- Nick Rixon, Private in the FDG
- Edwin, Private in the FDG

The War Axe

- Captain Micky San Marino
- Commander Suresha - Engines
- Commander MacEachthighearna (Mac) – Environmental
- Commander Blagun Lagunov – Structure
- Commander Oscar Wirth – Stores
- Lieutenant K'thrall, Yollin – Bridge Crew

The AssPlesius

- P'tok – captain of the Yollin raiding ship, the Singlaxian Grandeur

PROLOGUE

If you have not read the Terry Henry Walton Chronicles, then this short bit will catch you up. If you have read those books, then continue to Chapter One.

Gateway to the Universe is the first book that sets the stage for that which follows – four new and unique series set within the Age of Expansion, in the Kurtherian Gambit Universe.

- Craig Martelle will continue the adventures of Terry & Char (from the Terry Henry Walton Chronicles) in The Bad Company
- Justin Sloan will continue Valerie's adventures (from the Reclaiming Honor series) in Valerie's Elites
- JN Chaney and Sarah Noffke are writing the Ghost Squadron, continuing adventures of the FDG twenty years after Terry brings his warriors to the Federation

The first Vampire, Michael had been converted by the futuristic alien technology in a crashed Kurtherian ship. Through the power of the Pod Doc, nanocytes were injected into his body, changing him as the Kurtherian programming deemed. Over a thousand years later, at the start of the 21st century Michael introduced Bethany Anne to the technology, and she became his mate, one of the greatest of them all. Together they brought justice to the people. But fate separated them, and when the universe called to keep humanity safe, Bethany Anne had to take the fight to the stars before they could be reunited.

Bethany Anne left Earth before the World's Worst Day Ever (WWDE). Some called it the fall. Some called it the coming of the second dark ages.

While Bethany Anne became Empress of the Etheric Empire somewhere deep in Yol space, Earth was on its own. The WWDE had marked the beginning of a new era on Earth—the time of Terry Henry Walton and his struggle to drag humanity back to civilization.

Terry Henry—TH to his friends—had been discovered by Bethany Anne in Antarctica, using his body to keep another alive. She recognized him for what he was, a warrior for peace, and she personally authorized his enhancement. He later established the Force de Guerre, or FDG.

At the beginning, it was five men strong. Then, the Werewolf, Charumati, joined them.

Werewolves, those with receptive DNA who had received Kurtherian nanocytes, were able to change form in an instant. They healed at an incredible rate. They could see into the Etheric dimension and draw power from it.

They were special, just like TH. He had been enhanced with nanocytes, too, though he wasn't a Were.

Terry collected Werewolves, Weretigers, and even two Vampires as he built his FDG in an effort to rid the world of those who would oppress others, keep freedom out of their reach. Terry Henry and Char's family grew. They adopted Kimber and Kaeden. They had a child of their own, the gifted Cordelia. Together with their spouses, they formed an inner circle and they fought as one against evil.

Michael returned to Earth ahead of Bethany Anne. He found the Vampire Valerie and at his request, she did her part in bringing honor back to the world. With Robin, also a Vampire, they carved a path through the forces of evil.

When Bethany Anne returned to Earth one hundred and fifty years after the WWDE, she sent the FDG to space to ensure that her empire remained strong. The Empire that had become a Federation because she didn't believe in enslaving others. Neither did Terry Henry or his Werewolf wife.

The Etheric Federation needed the FDG to help the member planets do the right thing, even if it wasn't what they wanted to do. At Michael's request, Valerie and Robin joined the FDG, to do their part for the Empress.

Terry and Char would find new allies as they took their place in the universe, delivering humankind's single greatest export.

Justice.

CHAPTER ONE

A massive ship orbited planet Earth. Crewed by humans, aliens and a sentient artificial intelligence. The *ArchAngel II*. Larger than most asteroids, but with a singular purpose. To serve humanity.

One human in particular. Bethany Anne, *The Etheric Empress*.

The ambassadorial ship, little more than a luxury shuttle, departed the ArchAngel, followed by a squadron of fighters flying cover for the Empress as she and her mate Michael transferred to a Defender-series destroyer.

They needed the heavy lift that the ship *War Axe* provided if they were to free the trapped Elites.

As soon as the shuttle pod entered the landing bay, the destroyer pointed its nose toward the planet and headed into the upper atmosphere. It skipped and bounced as it became a fireball during its steep descent.

The captain had discussed the best way to inform those below on the planet that there was a new power, and half the world saw the harbinger flaming through the sky.

The *War Axe* left space and raced through Earth's sky at a speed in excess of Mach 30.

The ship slowed as it approached the island of Japan where Akio waited in a pod, hovering a half-mile above a collapsed building that he had protected for the past one hundred and fifty years. Eight stories deep, under a hundred thousand tons of rubble, six Elite warriors had been awakened from their deep sleep, slowing their aging. They had been buried inadvertently, back when chaos ruled.

Even their magnificent skills couldn't stop the madness. And Akio could not save them without risking their lives.

So, he had waited. With infinite patience, Akio, Yuko, and Eve protected both their world, and their team. Vampires with a sense of duty and honor, because the Queen, now an Empress, had tasked them to hold the line.

Keep the world from destroying itself.

They almost failed.

But Akio had found help. Former Marine Terry Henry Walton and his Werewolf partner joined forces with the Vampire to drag humanity back to civilization, a one hundred and fifty-year effort.

That chapter was *quickly coming to a close.*

The *War Axe* descended, slowing as the gravitic engines surged to control the bulk of the ship. Akio directed the ship to the building and then pulled his pod back. The Defender-series ship had the latest in traction beams. Using all the power available to it, the ship latched on to the building and picked it up en masse.

The rubble of a destroyed building held together by the

power of the energy beam. The ship slid sideways and dumped the building into a clear area beyond.

Akio's pod, a small and boxy ship to shuttle troops and equipment from planet-side to orbit, swooped above the hole in the ground, stopping mid-air and descending straight down. One hundred feet deep, the pod settled and the rear ramp dropped. Six Vampires stood there, waiting. Akio stepped out, bowing deeply to his fellows.

"It has been too long," he told them.

"Hai!" one of them said with a big smile. They hurried anxiously onto the shuttle, as if a delay would condemn them to be buried anew. Akio instructed Eve, an Artificial Intelligence within a body made of a seamless material not of Earth, to land aboard the *War Axe*.

The Empress was waiting.

San Francisco

Terry Henry Walton, TH to his friends, stood tall and proud, his black Force de Guerre uniform crisp. The Werewolf, Charumati, watched him, her eyes sparkling purple in the morning sun. They were anxious, excited, and afraid. None of them knew what to expect, and they all had different ideas.

A massive and fantastic vessel approached from the west, just like Akio had told him it would.

Akio, a Queen's Bitch, one of the chosen few to do the Empress's bidding from the time when she was *only* a queen.

TH caught Char's wince out of the corner of his eye. He reached for her hand, to hold it, look adoringly into her sparkling purple eyes, as he often did, and asked, "What's wrong?"

"So many from the Unknown World feeding off the power of the etheric," she replied, wrinkles appearing around her eyes as she fought against the pain.

The etheric, an alternate dimension from which the Kurtherians drew power for the nanocytes they invented. The nanos that coursed through the blood of all the enhanced and modified--the Were, the boosted, and the Vampires. *Especially* the Vampires. They were the most different of the enhanced. They were also the first ones to come alive from the specific Kurtherian technology which supported Bethany Anne's herself.

Joseph and his wife Petricia stayed close to Terry as he'd asked them to. It was his turn to protect them, payback for all the times they had his back. Joseph and Petricia were known as Forsaken, the Vampires created that left Michael's family, went on their own. For most, who didn't know Michael's strictures, you were *by default* Forsaken. The Elites, the special warriors, were unforgiving on the Forsaken, hunting them down and killing them, as Terry himself had often done. But Joseph and Petricia were different. They refused to drink human blood.

But Terry Henry and these two Forsaken had fought, side by side. TH considered them his friends and would stand by them, no matter what judgment came. Joseph had joined Char's pack well over a century earlier. As the Werewolf pack's alpha, she would vouch for the Forsaken, as she'd vouch for the Weretigers in the pack.

It wasn't a normal Werewolf pack, but nothing about TH and Char's life could have been considered normal.

The nanocytes coursing through their blood and the blood of their children eliminated any chance of the mundane. The nanos granted long life, repaired injuries, increased speed, and enhanced strength. Made warriors like Terry Henry Walton into super warriors.

But TH and Char made themselves into something far beyond anything the Kurtherians contemplated. Their joining made them stronger than the sum of their two parts. They made for a lethal combination.

Bethany Anne and Michael. The universe's premier beings--one had lived through death itself and the other, Bethany Anne, had cast off the Kurtherian yoke from their planet and others, freeing countless humans and aliens.

Liberty for all.

For Bethany Anne, it was simple: she hated bullies. The Kurtherians had been a race of bullies. When they collided with BA, the very stars eventually shuddered at the impact.

The Kurtherians she encountered lost because humanity would not be denied and mankind's champion *refused* to lose. The love of her life would be waiting for her, but she had to survive and return to Earth. And now she was back.

She was back with Michael by her side, and the universe breathed a sigh of relief.

The *War Axe* descended slowly, regally. They had cleared the transshipment area of the wharf for the ship to land, but had underestimated the vast proportions of such a vessel.

"This ship is a gnat compared to the ArchAngel," Terry said excitedly. Char clenched her jaw as she struggled with the energies ebbing and surging from those aboard the ship.

Terry looked at the assembled group of his friends and family. He nodded toward them.

Most didn't notice.

Marcie winced and gasped. Colonel Marcie Walton, Terry and Char's daughter-in-law, married to their adopted son Kaeden, a major in the FDG. Marcie had been gifted nanocytes from her mother, Felicity, one of the enhanced.

Felicity was nearby, holding the hand of her Werewolf husband, torn between watching the ship and comforting her daughter. She chose the latter, moving close and draping a protective arm over Marcie's shoulder.

Felicity and Marcie were both raving beauties, blonde hair and blue eyes, lithe. Felicity was a socialite, but Marcie had chosen a different path. She had found her niche. She was a *warrior's* warrior, the deadliest of the deadly.

Terry and Char's adopted daughter Kimber put a hand on her brother Kae's arm. The family had always been close. More than a century had passed, but time didn't matter.

Family did.

Kae nodded to his sister. More than family, they were friends, too. And brothers-in-arms, having fought side by side against the enemies of mankind. It was what their father had instilled in their souls, without pushing them into it. Having the ability to act, they accepted the responsibility. Terry was proud they'd followed his path, but more than that, they followed him as the leader of the FDG, embracing his moral compass as the right way to live.

Kim's husband Auburn was enhanced, too, because she couldn't abide watching her husband grow old, which was the curse of the enhanced. When he turned sixty, he went into the pod doc and even though it wasn't to the level of the one Bethany Anne used, he still came out a young thirty-five. He was the logistics chief for the FDG. He wouldn't fight, that wasn't his thing, but he could make sure everyone had their gear, and he could raise cattle.

His family ran the stockyards outside Chicago. He wondered how many cattle would fit aboard the ship before him. If they were going to space, he wanted steak to take the edge off, as he had explained to the others, but they hadn't been listening.

Terry and Char's natural daughter, Cordelia, and her husband Ramses tried to see past the others. They settled for a spot next to Joseph and Petricia. Cory had been special from the moment she was born. It was rare for Werewolf bitches to give birth and virtually unheard of with a human partner. Cory glanced at her parents, feeling how they radiated love. It was how she had grown up. She had never lost her appreciation for it, or taken their love for granted.

Cory had the gift of healing. She could 'encourage' her nanocytes to heal others. She'd even healed Akio at one point, but some of his nanocytes had flooded back into her bloodstream. From that point forward, her eyes glowed blue. She wore sunglasses when they took her on night operations, unless they needed to use her like a flashlight.

She wasn't too keen on that.

Charumati's pack was there as well. Standing farther away from the ship, away from the Vampires.

Sue, Timmons, Shonna, and Merrit shuffled impatiently. Two mated Werewolf pairs. They fought for their alpha. They fought for their friends.

The Weretigers, Aaron and Yanmei, were relaxed in the company of the Werewolves. The pack had been together for a long time, exactly one hundred years since Yanmei joined.

Ripples across the etheric were hitting the most sensitive of them like waves slapping against a beach.

A lower hatch on the ship opened and a stairway unfolded itself to the ground.

Akio walked out first. Terry exhaled heavily. He hadn't realized he'd been holding his breath. Char released his hand and wiped the sweat on her pants.

She moved in closer and wrapped her arm around Terry's waist. He turned and kissed the side of her head. When he looked back, he saw that Akio had been joined by six others.

Char recoiled as they approached. Terry had guessed that they were the Elites who had been trapped.

Now he was sure.

Akio stopped and the Elites fanned out behind him. Akio bowed deeply, deeper than ever before. Terry and Char bowed together, to a perfect ninety-degree angle. Terry and Char's children bowed. They'd spent a great deal of time in Japan with Akio and Yuko when they had received the nanocytes by way of Akio's Pod Doc.

A long time had passed since then, but they had not forgotten their manners or their respect for Akio. The Vampire stood up straight before approaching and shaking hands with Terry and then Char. Akio waved awkwardly to the people standing around.

Cory smiled widely and waved back.

The Elites remained stoic. They had been freed earlier that day, and were happy to be anywhere other than their underground prison, but they were still getting used to people and regenerating from the massive energy Michael had bestowed upon them, personally shoving energy into their nanocytes, making them come alive and rejuvenating their bodies.

A group left the ship, strolling casually toward TH and Char. The Elites stepped aside, creating a tunnel through which they could pass. A dark-haired beauty walked at the side of a man who wore a long black coat. His eyes took in everything while remaining focused on Terry Henry.

They stopped before passing the last of their Vampire escorts. The woman's eyes glowed red. She glanced from one face to the next, stopping at Joseph. Her lip pursed a moment of their own accord, pausing as she considered the Forsaken.

TH stepped between them, drawing the attention of the Elites. Their hands seized pistol grips and sword hilts. Terry held his hands up.

The man chuckled silently. The shorter woman smiled crookedly.

"We've met before, Empress," Terry said. He dropped to one knee and bowed his head before continuing. "I'm sorry. Akio asked us to help him prepare this world for your return, and I've failed him. I've failed you."

Char stepped forward and put a hand on her husband's back. Her eyes glistened. It was supposed to be a joyous return, but TH, as he always did, took responsibility for everything, whether in his control or not.

"Cut the Empress bullshit, Terry, I remember you from the Antarctica operation. You were in hypothermia, if I remember correctly, before you were put in the Pod Doc. I'm Bethany Anne to you and I'd like to introduce Michael," she said, taking in the sights and sounds of San Francisco. "Things look pretty damn good from where I'm standing." She turned to the purple-eyed woman next to TH and winked. "And you must be Char."

Bethany Anne held out her hand, no hint of subterfuge. "Trust me, behind every strong man is a strong woman." There was a snort from behind Bethany Anne, who caught the slight glint of humor in Char's eyes from Michael's unsaid comment.

"I am. Pleased to meet you, Empress," Char replied, taking BA's warm hand and shaking firmly.

Bethany Anne rolled her eyes. "Oh for fuck's sake, stand up, TH! You're making me feel weird." Terry stood as she eyed him. "And don't apologize again. It would be pretty embarrassing for me to kick your ass upside-down and sideways in front of your wife and kids. For the record, I trust *you*. If you trust *your people*, I trust your people." BA nodded toward Joseph and Petricia.

"I trust them with my life," Terry said.

Bethany Anne nodded. "Listen up, people," she said, projecting her voice to be heard for those without enhanced hearing. "Would you stop looking like a police academy cadet review?" She nodded them forward. "Come here and let's talk like people who have kicked some ass and now are going to get a little R and R."

The group hesitated, but Char waved them over. Felicity dragged Ted toward the front of the mob. She looked down and stopped abruptly, grinning.

She pointed. "I just love those boots!" Felicity exclaimed in her southern drawl.

Bethany Anne put up a finger to stop the next comment she just knew Michael was straining to keep in. "I know, right? Finally! A woman with taste." She turned to him. "See? It's all about the shoes."

"San Francisco has some of the best shopping in the world if you can spare a few minutes," Felicity replied.

Bethany Anne looked up at Michael. He struggled mightily, his jaws working as he grimaced, before surrendering and letting his eyes roll.

"And he'll go, too," BA said. "I've been away from this hunk of mostly hairless hot stuff for way too long."

Michael pursed his lips and commented, "It's growing. It's just taking a while."

She watched as the group formed a semicircle around her. "I wanted to meet you personally and *thank* you for everything you've done both in my name and on your own to help make the world a better place. Akio said that he could not have chosen better, even if he had a choice." She paused a moment before continuing, "What we've found across the universe is that no matter how hard we try, evil will never be defeated."

She shrugged. "It can be stomped into the ground." Bethany Anne put up her fingers, just an inch apart. "It can be sliced into little fucking pieces, but where one is removed, another takes its place. Fucking cockroaches all! We can relegate them to the dark places, the slime and swamps in which they breed, but they'll always be there. No matter. You helped make the world safe for humanity once again. You carved a chunk out of life's cesspool and you handed it over so they could make their own way. Self-determination and all that."

She sighed. "And now you have some choices. One of which is to take the rest you deserve. God knows you deserve it and you will absolutely receive it if that is what you want." She smiled a moment. "However." She winked at Terry Henry. "You knew there was going to be a however, right?"

She received the chuckles she was looking for. "I want to invite you to take the *War Axe* through the Annex Gate and join my father in securing and expanding the brand new Etheric Federation. There is a little side business called The Bad Company that I think you and your people would be *perfect* to slide right into. What do you think about exporting justice to the universe, TH?" BA didn't wait for an answer before continuing.

She pointed up. "The sky beckons the warriors. Come home to me, TH. Earth will survive without you, because you taught it to. You've done your duty. Your legacy will live on, but I have a new mission ready for those willing to step up. To take your skills and get-shit-done attitude in a place that will cause your eyes to pop out. Come home to the stars. Come home to the Etheric Federation." She looked over the group. "*All of you.*"

Terry squeezed Char's hand. They turned and smiled at each other. He looked at the rest of the eager faces. It was everything he never knew that he wanted. He opened his mouth to speak…

Before he could answer, a huge German Shepard-looking dog vaulted from the ship and raced in a wide arc around the Elites and slid to a stop near Terry and Char, wagging its tail furiously as it looked at him.

"Who's a good boy?" Terry said, wearing a ridiculous grin as he took in the dog. Char tried to keep her face calm with her husband who just couldn't stop himself.

Michael answered. "He knows who the good boy is. This is Dokken, and he's pretty smart. When and if you get a chip in your head, you'll be able to communicate with him," Michael finished before turning to the panting creature. "Yes? Are you sure? Okay. Have it your way," Michael said aloud, speaking to the dog. He looked back to TH. "He says to tell you that he thinks you're a good boy, too."

Terry started to laugh, in a way that a person does when they're among friends.

CHAPTER TWO

O n Board the *ArchAngel II*

Valerie and Robin emerged from the transport ship, closely following Michael as he led them into the *ArchAngel II*, the large ship they had seen from the ground when Michael picked them up.

It was still almost unbelievable that Valerie had left her friends behind, all but Robin.

The woman at her side, barely a woman at all if you counted her actual age instead of looking at her through the lens of all she had done.

Now it was the two of them leaving the comfort of their homes behind to go off and join Michael in the fight for humanity's survival from a different angle—from space.

Only, as Michael had just explained to them, they had signed up for more than anything they could have fathomed before his explanation.

Most impressive, and exciting, among those was that they were about to meet the Bethany Anne, or BA, as some called her. If Cammie could've been here, she would've pissed her pants in excitement, at least just a little. Valerie, for that matter, was pleasantly surprised it wasn't happening yet.

Everything she had heard about BA was a confusing smorgasbord of one part awesome with a major portion of confusion thrown in for good measure. She was pretty sure most of the horrible parts were lies.

Valerie's understanding of Bethany Anne was a picture painted of the legend by Vampires she had been raised with back before she broke off from them to stop her brother's invasion of America. Then she had met Michael and become his Justice Enforcer, and come to understand that much she thought she knew about the world were fabrications...*lies*.

That included Bethany Anne.

She wasn't the devil many had believed her to be, but more like a take-no-shit woman who had risen up to take control of Weres and Vampires in Michael's absence, and then taken the fight to space. Her focus was on saving humanity.

At this moment, Valerie couldn't imagine any more respect and admiration could possibly be flowing out of her and toward Bethany Anne. Her hands were almost shaking with nerves and excitement as they approached, and Michael had to even turn and give her a calming glance before they entered the great reception room aboard *ArchAngel II*.

"Remember," he told them, "she is your empress now, but she is also a warrior, just like you. A woman given power beyond belief, who fights for justice. You aren't so different, at the end of the day. I can assure you, she still puts her pants on one leg at a time."

Valerie felt the heat rush to her cheeks. "I-I'm not usually like this…"

He raised an eyebrow. "What, like a gushing school girl from when we had boarding schools?" Michael asked. If he was trying to hide the smile pulling at the edge of his lips, he wasn't doing a clever job of it. "I know. However, trust me, you needn't be nervous." He glanced over. "Nor you, Robin."

It was only then that Valerie noticed how pale Robin was.

For her friend, Valerie pulled herself together. She stood a bit taller, chest out, jaw clenched, and nodded. At her side, Robin worked to do the same.

He looked them both over and nodded slightly. "Very good." Michael motioned for them to follow, and then led the way through the last set of sliding metal doors.

As they entered, a team of men and women turned to assess them. Each was intimidating in their own way, but all even more so because of the scent Valerie was catching —there was certainly something of Vampire and Were here, though it was different. Like nothing she had ever engaged.

They slowly parted and Valerie was able to see her. She seemed taller, but Valerie noticed her boots…had heels?

Bethany Anne was speaking to a man who she had to look up at even in heels. He was shaking his head, and Valerie could hear their conversation.

"Look, John." Bethany Anne was talking. "If we have one fucking chance of locating a cache, imagine the stories we could tell for centuries." Her hands were animated, moving apart.

"BA, I'm with William. I can't believe--regardless of the stories we both heard when we were here on Earth before--that there are *any* Twinkies still edible on this whole planet."

Bethany Anne sighed, her shoulders slumping just a bit. "Well, that fucking sucks." The movement around her broke their conversation and Bethany Anne's head turned to her left, a small smile playing on her lips as the two women came closer.

At the sight of her watching them, both Valerie and Robin bent to one knee instinctively.

"Empress, we are honored to serve," Valerie stated, still not looking up.

Without even the sound of footsteps, she was aware that Bethany Anne was standing directly in front of her. A finger met her chin, pulling her up to look upon the Empress, then a nod to tell her to stand.

"Welcome to the ArchAngel and welcome to standing among those who fight for Earth. Whether from out in space--" She pointed up. "--or here on the planet. You have my appreciation and respect for all you have done. Both before you met Michael, and since." She looked at him. "Although showing up like he did in a lightning storm with Forsaken all around and your brother trying to kill you was a bit much."

"The timing *was* impressive," Michael agreed.

All Valerie and Robin could do was look at each other in confusion, which made Bethany Anne and Michael both start chuckling and a few others seemed to be enjoying the camaraderie in a way she couldn't yet understand.

It was like these two had just walked into some old members only club and had a lot to learn.

"Don't worry," Bethany Anne told them with a wave of her hand. "You'll learn to fit right in. As for now…" She glanced around at the others there. "We'll need a few minutes alone."

The others nodded and departed with welcoming nods to Valerie and Robin.

When it was just Bethany Anne, Michael, Valerie, and Robin, Bethany Anne stepped closer and took each of the women in an embrace. She pulled back, eyeing them, and smiled, a bit of her earlier humor in her eyes lost and concern replacing it. "You two have no idea what you're getting into, do you?"

Valerie glanced around at the ship, wondering where it had been and what it had seen, and turned back to Bethany Anne, "None."

Robin shook her head.

"Fair enough." Bethany Anne nodded and started pacing as she spoke. "The future is going to be treacherous, but *beautiful*. Mind-blowingly full of activity, and yet, you'll have moments where you wonder what you're doing with your life and how you got here." She sighed. "Unfortunately, your heart will ache as you miss your friends here on Earth. I can promise you that as I still ache a couple of times a year as I think of friends who died almost two centuries ago."

Bethany Anne turned and walked the other way. "On the positive side, you will meet friends of entirely new species, species or races or whatever they are of aliens that you've never been able to even imagine…and some of them might become your new best friends." She stopped to look at the two women, letting this sink in for a moment. "Do you understand this? *Can* you understand this?"

Valerie's heart fluttered and her throat went dry, but she nodded.

"If I may," Robin said, surprising Valerie. The others turned, waiting patiently. "We've proven ourselves on Earth," the young woman continued, "and we've done what we can to get it, or at least our immediate area, the closest to order and peace that we thought possible. Maybe it will last, maybe it won't, but…I think we both understand that there's a much larger war going on up here, and if we stayed on Earth, not being a part of it, well, we might as well be dead."

"I think she means to say," Valerie jumped in, not fond of the ending of her friend's little speech, "is that it would be no worse than crawling into some hole and just sleeping through it all. We aren't that type of women. If there's a problem, you can bet this spaceship that we'll be on the front line working to shove that problem's head up his own ass."

"Spaceship," Michael said, smiling. "That's a *cute* way of referring to the *ArchAngel II*."

There was a female's voice, one that sounded like Bethany Anne but came from the speakers in the room. "I am a Leviathan Class Super-Dreadnought, built in the space yards of the Yollin Fleet. I am the first of my kind and if I can take a quote from a movie, I've seen things you people wouldn't believe. Attack ships on fire off the shoulder of Orion. I watched C-beams glitter in the dark near the Tannhäuser Gate. All those moments I will add to, like tears in the rain. It is not yet my *second* time to die."

It was clear Bethany Anne was trying not to laugh, but she simply nodded and replied with, "*Good.*"

"Good?" Valerie pursed her lips, waiting for more. When nothing more came, she continued, "Good as in, you're happy to have us on board?"

Bethany Anne raised an eyebrow. "Of course! Please, your efforts preceded you. Had you fallen in your trials, we would have paid our respects and made sure that your coffin was sent into the sun at a minimum to our fallen warrior. Your names have already been written into the history books." She nodded, satisfied. "I'm looking forward to hearing about your contributions to the Bad Company."

"Actually," Michael started, but paused.

Bethany Anne looked over. "Yes?"

Michael replied, "Well, the discussions have revolved around her forming a new team."

Because?

She's a bit of a loner. She does not know how to fit in the bigger group. Between her and Robin, they tend not to want the dust to settle under their asses for too long.

Bethany Anne's chuckle was easy to hear in their mind speech. *Yes, I know the type well.* She turned back to the two.

"We shall go with Valerie's Elites, then, a team working under the Bad Company." Bethany Anne looked between the two and winked. "It's a hell of a name, make sure you step up your game."

Michael gestured to the doors and nodded. "Come, we'll get someone to show you to the shuttle while Bethany

Anne and I chat. You'll need to transfer over to the *War Axe* as soon as possible. You'll want to introduce yourselves and make yourselves at home. It's going to be a long journey, and you will want to get to know everyone."

They walked to the door and turned to once more thank him and Bethany Anne for including them in this, and then exited, both feeling as if they had just walked to Mount Olympus in a mythological Greece and stood among the gods.

CHAPTER THREE

On board the *War Axe*

Terry and Char turned their attention to the group in the ship's recreation room. No one had ventured beyond what they knew. Dokken stood at Terry's side, waiting patiently.

"You're going to scratch that dog's hair off," Char told her husband. Dokken cocked his head back and forth as he looked at the Werewolf. He started to growl, but she snapped her teeth at him, eyes sparking purple. She was the alpha.

The big dog backed up a step. "Hey!" Terry looked down at the massive German Shepard. Terry didn't have to bend down to pet his head. They both seemed to like that. "Don't be scaring my dog."

If a dog could sigh, Dokken pulled it off magnificently.

"Sorry, buddy," Terry apologized. He looked into the rec room where two platoons of FDG warriors were waiting. Terry and Char, then their kids, had spent the majority of their adult lives serving in one military or another. Thousands had served in the Force de Guerre over the years, but they'd reduced the numbers of those in active service to what Terry looked at.

One hundred percent had volunteered to follow Colonel Walton to space. He didn't expect that, but when it happened, it was a mad scramble to bring everyone aboard the *War Axe*, which wasn't family friendly, but the warriors with families came regardless. The destroyer's crew went out of their way to make the newcomers feel welcome.

But they had so much to learn. None of them had operated in space before. None of them had met an alien before, until they boarded the *War Axe*, where they met a few Yollins.

Yollins were the galaxy's warriors. Some with two legs, some with four, and mandibles, they were sufficiently foreign to Earth's humans to shock their senses. Terry Henry thought he was ready to meet them, but he wasn't. And neither were any of the others. Cory was the kindest of them all and greeted them warmly, but without their chips, the translators installed, none of Terry Henry or his people could communicate with the aliens.

Or with Dokken.

"Listen up!" Terry bellowed into the crowd of confused people. There was nothing like getting the *word*. Right now, no one carried the power of the *word*. Without the *word*, the warriors filled in the gap in their knowledge with the worst things they could contemplate.

Terry couldn't have that. Char's concern told him that she also craved the *word*, just like him. That sealed it.

"I shall venture forth on a holy quest!" he yelled with a

big smile. Char's expression turned to one of disbelief. She rolled her eyes and shook her head.

"I will find out what our next steps are. We are traveling to the stars, but what will we need to learn along the way? I will publish a plan of the day and all of you--" He eyed the Weres specifically. "--will be sitting pretty and paying attention. Now stand by to stand by. Hurry up and wait! I'll be back as soon as I can find my way to the captain."

Everyone looked at TH. He looked back. He threw his hands over his head. "Hip, hip!"

He was greeted by silence.

"You yell 'hooray.' One more time," he snarled, not amused by the lack of gusto. "Hip, hip!"

"Hooray!" most of them offered with little feeling.

"Again!" he yelled. On the fourth round, they were on their feet and screaming 'hooray.' Terry was pleased.

"So say we all," he said softly to Char. She had to smile as she wondered how much television he was going to watch, now that it was available to him again with all his favorite shows from a long-gone era.

Dokken trotted toward the hatch and Terry and Char followed him out. He turned left, when Terry expected him to go right. They continued down the corridor, through multiple hatches, up a level, and through two more hatches before the dog stopped at a nondescript doorway.

"This reminds me of a submarine," Terry said. Char had been in the Navy at one point in her long life, and she recognized the similarities, too.

"Either get crushed or drowned or lose atmosphere and die in the vacuum of space," she intoned.

"Humans are so frail," Terry said with a chuckle. He and

Char were anything but. "What's in here, Dokken? Damn, I wish I could talk with you."

Terry scratched the German Shepard's ears. The door slid aside and a man stepped out. He looked quizzically at Terry and Char, before looking at Dokken and nodding.

"Follow me," the man said, turning and heading back into the room that looked like a mix between a high-end computer operation center and a medical laboratory.

"Why?" Terry asked, standing his ground.

"I thought you were sent here to get your upgrades? You'll need them if you want to communicate with Dokken, the ship, the Yollins, well, anyone. I can't imagine not being able to communicate," the man said.

"Isn't that what we're doing now?" Terry said, feeling the smartass in him rising. It had been a long time since someone had dismissed him as a lesser being. Char put out a restraining hand.

A voice bellowed from behind them. "Just fucking do it. Go in and take your medicine."

Terry turned at the words, narrowing his eyes at the man's face. Something looked familiar. Terry was getting ready to bark back at the man, but Char's gentle touch stayed his hand. He took a deep breath.

"I'm Terry Henry Walton, TH to my friends," Terry said, stepping forward with his hand outstretched.

The other man took it and gripped, firmly. Terry Henry smiled and leaned into his grip, recognizing the man's enhanced strength. He saw the light armor that the man wore. Exotic. Custom. Alien.

"I'm John Grimes," the man answered simply.

Terry lessened his grip in surprise at hearing the name.

His hand crunched as John squeezed for an instant before letting go. Terry winced, but held the man's eyes. "Mrs. Grimes was a member of my team. She was good people." Terry recognized that the two had the same shape and color of eyes.

"She was my cousin. I heard that you had taken care of her, helped her to live a long and happy life."

Terry racked his brain and couldn't come up with anyone who would have known that. Maybe Akio had been in Terry's mind more times than he let on. There wasn't much Terry could do about it now. He shook his head.

"Thank you, TH," John said sincerely before slapping Terry hard enough on the shoulder to knock down a lesser being.

"Candy-ass," Terry said softly with a half-smile. John ignored him as he turned to Char.

"You must be the power behind the throne, Charumati, alpha of your pack." She offered her hand, ready for a short power grip, but John bent down and kissed her long fingers instead. Dokken sneezed and shook his whole body.

"Only a Marine would do that to another Marine's wife." Terry took a bold step forward. Char looked at TH and then at John.

"Don't make me kick both your asses. A squid beating up on two Marines would be embarrassing for both of you. And if you win, then you're beating up a helpless young girl, but if I win, I'll be a legend."

Terry and John looked at each other. "And that's why I'm so in love after all these years."

John Grimes started to laugh, before looking at Dokken and twisting his mouth sideways. "I know, I know. It's so unlike me to do the foofy crap, but you're right, we have a schedule to keep. Come on, you two. Let's get you fixed up."

"I didn't know I was broken," Terry replied.

"It's all relative. I can't wait to spar with you. Maybe you'll give me a little something I haven't seen before. Probably not, but hey! We won't know until an ass is kicked, will we?"

Terry chuckled. He had an idea who John Grimes was because of conversations with Akio, but hadn't realized how much he would like the man. It was like he reconnected with a long-lost brother from his Marine Corps days.

"And you'll want to talk with him. He knows some shit." John jabbed a thumb toward Dokken.

Terry motioned for Char to go first and he followed her in. There was only one Pod Doc and there was a brief delay as Terry and Char looked at each other, trying to decide who would go first. They both pointed to the other and said, "You first," simultaneously.

"For fuck's sake. It'll take ten minutes. You first, TH, while I discuss with Charumati what it's like to live with a fucking jarhead for, what, a hundred years?"

"One twenty-eight, but who's counting." Char smirked.

"Goddammit!" Terry exclaimed while the man in the lab-coat tapped his foot impatiently. "Fine."

Terry climbed in and the Artificial Intelligence known as ArchAngel from the ship in orbit linked with the EI from the *War Axe* in order to install and optimize Terry's chip. Surreptitiously, the Pod Doc downloaded a sample of Terry's nanocytes for analysis, to determine what made them so special.

Ten minutes later, the Pod Doc opened and Terry hurried out. "Feels weird," he said as he smacked the side of his head.

Does my good boy's head hurt? Terry heard. It sounded like it was directly in his brain. He wasn't sure he'd heard anything. *Down here, dipstick.*

"I'll be damned. That's you, isn't it?" Terry asked Dokken.

No shit. Do you wonder why they told you I was the smart one? Because of questions like that.

"I've been wondering this my whole life. How do you know what you're going to pee on?" Terry asked the dog.

Dokken licked his dog lips and yawned, then started sniffing Terry's leg purposefully.

"Oh no you don't." Terry backed away, almost running into Char as she climbed into the Pod Doc. He mumbled an apology as the door closed, leaving Terry alone with John Grimes and Dokken.

"I'm going to have to go. You'll be able to talk with Smedley, the ship's EI. He'll get you where you need to go." John held out his hand. Terry's had already healed from the previous bone-crushing exchange, but this time, they shook like friends, not competitors.

"One thing, John. The word," Terry said, cocking his head. "My people are in the rec room, and I want to tell them what's going on. Can you tell me?"

"Just talk with Smedley, TH. He'll take care of it. I look forward to that sparring match, brother. Maybe you'll last longer than two seconds." John Grimes laughed as he rolled his shoulders in anticipation of the contest.

"Maybe, John. Until then." Terry nodded curtly, then pursed his lips. "Smedley?"

"Yeah, Smedley Butler, Marine Corps Medal of Honor recipient. I thought it fitting." John started to leave, stopped for a second, and spoke over his shoulder. "Family is everything, TH. You did my family a solid, and if you ever need anything, you give me a shout."

Terry watched the man leave. John walked like a warrior, alert, ready to react at any moment, even on a ship that should have been safe to all on board.

But Marines like John Grimes and Terry Henry Walton couldn't turn it off. They ran at high rpms.

All the time.

Dragging humanity back to civilization never took a day off. Neither did exporting justice.

"Smedley?" Terry asked cautiously.

>>Yes, Terry Henry Walton. You need something?<<

Holy crap! That is weird. And delightful. It tickles my nose. I have a question, Smedley, well, a number of questions. What's next for my people? I'd like to publish the plan of the day, so they know what is happening in their lives. It's important.

>>I will be more than happy to share a schedule with them, if you'd like. <<

What does the schedule look like?

Smedley directed him to a nearby monitor. A schedule of names and appointments appeared along with meal times, work out times, and even a recommended training regimen.

"I like it," Terry said aloud. "No choice about getting upgraded?"

"Not if they want to communicate," Smedley replied through the speakers next to the monitor.

"There you are!" Terry blurted. "We'll ask them while there's still time for them to change their mind. How much longer are we going to be on the ground here?"

"I think we will leave in five minutes."

"Holy shit! Can you patch me in to the rec room?"

"Of course," Smedley replied.

CHAPTER FOUR

Terry Henry sat in a chair before the monitor. He could see the people in the rec room. "Coming to you live, from the next stop on your all-expense-paid cruise through the Gateway to the Universe," Terry said jovially.

"Did you want me to show that to the people in the rec room?" Smedley asked.

"Of course! What the hell did you think I was doing?"

"I'm kidding. They can hear you," Smedley replied.

"Even now?"

"Yes, of course."

"What the hell?" Terry looked at the speaker to the side of the screen, ignoring the group of people staring at him from the rec room. "You're not an AI, so you aren't supposed to have a sense of humor."

"But we are studying hard, TH. I go to AI night school to improve myself. ArchAngel runs sessions three times a week."

"Who the fuck are you?" Terry blurted.

"I'm Smedley Butler. Named after a Marine Corps Major General who was, at the time, the most decorated Marine in history. John Grimes thought it apropos because I am the *War Axe*, and my primary mission is combat. Will we be going to war soon? It is my purpose for being one with this ship."

Terry leaned back and whistled. "That's a damn good question, General. We'll try to get an answer to that, but not just for you," Terry said, turning toward the people on the screen, "but for all of you, too. Smedley, post the schedule for everyone to see. I'm sure they're tired of looking at my mug."

"I'm not," Char whispered from behind Terry's ear. He jumped and shook his head, before relaxing and looking at the people who had come with him from San Francisco.

"You'll see the time slots for each and every one of you for the Pod Doc. This is a medical procedure to install a communications chip of some sort in your head. It is perfectly safe and takes almost no time to do, but since this is your body, you can decide that you don't want it. Unfortunately, if you want to come along, it will be required as it gives us the ability to communicate with the ship and those whose language we don't speak."

Dokken appeared and stood on his back legs, putting his front paws on Terry's leg. He nodded to the screen. Char stood on the other side with her arm draped casually over Terry's shoulders.

"That means you, too," Char said, pointing at her pack and her family.

"Count me in," Marcie said.

"And me," Kaeden added as a chorus of cheers followed.

"Is there anyone who doesn't want the procedure or who wants to know more? There has to be someone." No one spoke or raised a hand. "Pull one of the officers aside if you want your privacy. It's okay. This isn't for everyone. That damn Smedley is in my head."

The German Shepard nudged his arm.

"And you, too, Dokken."

"You'll see on the schedule that half your day will be spent in one of two classrooms. Think about how big the universe is. We're playing catchup, people. We're in this together. Knowledge is power. We are sorely lacking right now, so these classes will be the most important thing we do for the next few weeks." Terry looked at the speaker. "Smedley. How long until we get where we're going?"

"I'm sure I can't answer that."

Terry cocked his head. Even Dokken looked at the screen in surprise.

"It's math. Aren't you supposed to be good at that stuff?"

"I can do the calculations, but I don't know to where you're referring. Do we have any more stops on Earth after this? No. Are we going to match orbits with the *ArchAngel II*? Yes, and transfer the executively royal passengers. Then we'll travel to the Annex Gate at best possible speed. Through the gate into Yol space, then conduct a second gate jump to the Onyx Station from which we'll embark a few specialists before a final jump to the Dren Cluster where I was told will be the base for your operations."

Terry's head swam with the locations. He didn't know where any of those places were.

"Show us a star chart with these locations highlighted."

Instantly, a starfield appeared. There was a huge yellow hand with 'you are here' written on a pointing finger. Terry sighed, but the image zoomed out and rotated, then zoomed back in to focus on that area. The image expanded and did a fly-through to the next stopping point.

The ship lurched almost imperceptibly as it took off.

"Did we miss our last chance for someone to change their mind on going into the Pod Doc?" Terry asked.

"People always change their mind, TH," Smedley said patiently while the group in the rec room continued to study the star charts that the EI displayed to orient them to Federation space. "But they can no longer leave the ship, unless they want to space themselves, jump out an airlock, as it may be."

"As it may be. I hope they were sincere in signing up. We shall see." Terry turned back to the main screen. "Colonel Marcie, Majors, the word has been given. Carry out the plan of the day. Walton out."

"Sign me off, General," Terry told the EI. The screen went blank. "What do you think, Dokken?"

Terry scratched the dog behind its ears as he smiled into Dokken's dog face.

You know you look pretty stupid when you do that, Dokken told him.

"I don't care, you butt-sniffing nematode," Terry replied matter-of-factly.

That's how it's going to be, huh? Name-calling is so passé, TH.

"Fine. Have it your way," Terry declared in a deep voice. "What's next, Dokken? Maybe you can take us to the captain of this tug?"

Sounds good. Dokken leaned into Terry's hand and twisted his head as the colonel's fingers found a good spot. The German Shepard dropped his front paws to the deck and shook vigorously. Terry stood and held out his hand. Char took it and they walked out, side by side, partners on the next phase of the journey.

"Looks like you guys are first," Marcie told the Weres and the Forsaken. Timmons looked closely at the list. Using a finger to stop the scrolling names and roll it back to the first group.

"And you," Timmons told Marcie.

She pointed to Kaeden, Kimber, Auburn, Cory, and Ramses. "And you guys. We're second." She pointed back to the pack. "Looks like you have about one minute to make your appointment. Better not be late."

Timmons and Sue took one last look at the map and strolled away. Timmons was first through the door and immediately turned right. The rest of the group chuckled.

"This way," Sue said, nodding to the left. Timmons looked both ways and grunted. He walked past the group with his head held high.

"You passed the test," he told them.

Shonna and Merrit followed, then Aaron, Yanmei, Joseph, and Petricia, with Ted and Felicity bringing up the rear.

"I'm not sure about this," Petricia whispered at Joseph.

"If it makes you feel any better, I'm not sure either, but we do what we must. If I'm to understand correctly, the

Pod Docs created the first of our kind and many since. We are the unsanctioned. But there are those like us who would follow Michael's strictures, if we only knew what they were."

Petricia shivered with worry. She remained uncertain and nothing Joseph could do would alleviate her concerns. He couldn't be reassuring when he was as in the dark as she was.

"I'll go first, my love," he said. It was his way, a way of life he'd been born into.

Chivalry lived on.

At least in Joseph's heart. Terry had done the same thing earlier. Even though the women didn't need protecting, that was how their men had always been and always would be. Char had protected Terry as often as he'd protected her. But she let him have his way.

When it suited her.

Petricia was much younger than Joseph, but who quibbles about the difference between a century or four? Joseph would have it no other way.

She opened her mouth to argue with him, but he smiled at her. Who was she to refuse that?

The group trudged through the hallway, walking markedly slower the closer they came to the space where the Pod Doc was located. The lab-coat wearing technician was waiting for them. His arms were crossed and his foot beat a staccato against the corridor's deck.

"I'm first," Marcie called as she approached, but Joseph rushed past the group.

"No. I'll go before the rest as I expect I'll be the most

challenging." Joseph took his wide brimmed hat off and looked at the man.

"I expect you will be," the technician replied after looking closely at the Forsaken. The man waved at the large group to follow him in. He did the math in his head. Fourteen people at roughly ten minutes each….

It would be a while before this group finished. He had expected them to come in smaller groups.

Joseph climbed into the Pod Doc and the door shut. Petricia and his friends watched the equipment silently. Less than half of them had gone through the process. Marcie, Kim, Kae, and Ramses had received the nanocytes and programming from Akio's Pod Doc, which was on its last leg.

The process that was taking ten minutes on the *War Axe* had taken them six months using the roughly-repaired older technology.

It was a new age. A better age where they would fly to the future on an alien ship with technologies they had never dreamed of.

Ted could go for weeks without talking to anyone, but here, he saw nirvana. "Can you explain the interface of this system, how it takes the person's data and reconfigures the nanos?" Ted asked as he looked at the computer station that the man occupied.

The technician only watched the status indicators on the screens. He wasn't interacting with process. Ted scratched his chin in wonder as he explored the possibilities.

"These upgrades are being handled by ArchAngel

herself," the man said with a smile. "Smedley is helping, too."

Ted nodded as his mind disappeared into the data streams scrolling in front of his eyes. The man was talking, but Ted didn't acknowledge him. Felicity tapped the technician on the shoulder.

"He can't hear you," she drawled.

"But, but…" the man stammered, pointing to Ted sitting two feet away.

"He can't. Trust me on this. We've been married for a long time. He has gone inside that magic box of yours. My husband may never return." Felicity looked forlornly at her Werewolf husband.

The latch clicked on the door to the Pod Doc.

You sumbitch! Dokken 'yelled' and took off running. He slid through a sharp corner and slammed into the wall before scrabbling to find purchase and dashing forward.

Terry and Char were in hot pursuit because they weren't sure where they were going. As long as their guide was running, they were running.

Dokken ran face-first into a door that slid closed right in front of him. He tore at the obstruction, ripping at it with his paws.

"What are you chasing?" Char asked.

That damn cat! He is my arch enemy, a nemesis the likes of which has not plagued humankind for untold centuries, Dokken declared.

"A cat," Char said slowly, putting her hands on her hips.

Terry reached for the panel beside the door. "What are you doing?"

"We're going after that cat!" Terry declared, looking determined.

"Why?"

"Because Dokken is my friend and he has an arch enemy somewhere beyond that door," Terry explained patiently, relaxing and smiling.

That's a good boy. Now use those thumbs of yours to open this door!

"Hey, buddy, I'm starved. Where do we eat? Did you know that we brought a few tons of real beef, the best on the planet?" Char asked the German Shepard.

What's beef? Dokken asked, turning his head back and forth as he looked at Char, the door behind him forgotten.

"Meat. Domestic, organic, possibly even orgasmic if you've never had it before. Weathers family nurtured. It's a treat better than any treat you've ever had before."

Better than bistok?

"I don't know what bistok is, but I suspect beef is better. You know what I am. When I'm in Were form, I can't get enough beef. It's like delicate fingers dancing over your tongue, sending joy directly into your brain."

I'm not sure what we're waiting for, Dokken said excitedly as he trotted off. Terry took Char's hand and they followed the dog, expecting that he knew where he was going.

A sound behind him said that a door had opened. An orange cat leaned out, casually licking a paw and wiping his face. Terry used his free hand to give the cat the finger.

Char looked at him, wondering.

"He's our arch nemesis," Terry stated firmly, tipping his head back for emphasis.

"Do you want me to change into a wolf and chase the scary kitty away?" Char said in her most concerned voice. Terry hesitated. "You're thinking about it!"

"Am not! But he's our arch nemesis."

"No. He's not. He's a cat and a dog doesn't like him, but can't be anything more than an arch enemy. An arch nemesis? That would have been Mister Smith, and things didn't end well for him."

Terry snarled. Mister Smith had haunted his dreams for decades, but when he, Akio, and the pack caught up with the Forsaken, Paris had trembled under the onslaught. Marcie had ended the Vampire's life with a keen sword stroke.

While Terry, Char, and the others watched. That was how most of the enemies in Terry's life had died. Defeated and whimpering. That made TH smile. He and Char were still alive and kicking.

And they had a dog again, even if he did talk back.

CHAPTER FIVE

Valerie and Robin walked through the corridors of the *War Axe*. Valerie carried her trusty sword—an old European blade passed down to her. A bracelet of simple silver glittered from Robin's wrist—a memento from her father, one he had given her after they had relocated in New York. They had taken the news of her going into space quite well, considering the fact they had lost their daughter once to Vampires before finding her again.

When she had explained the reason for her going this time, they had nodded, given her the bracelet, and made her promise to bring their alien enemies hell.

Valerie still wondered if they had understood what Robin was getting into. Hell, she wondered if she really understood it herself. She had a feeling this was going to be one crazy ride.

Other than that, they carried nothing from their old lives. What use did they have of old belongings in space?

They followed the directions that Michael had given them and arrived at the recreation room. Inside, they found two platoons from Colonel Walton's Force de Guerre—FDG—milling about, working out, waiting.

One face in particular was a welcome sight to Valerie. There, in the middle of the recreation room, was Sergeant Garcia. The man had been sent by Colonel Walton to help set up New York's military, but had stayed and done more for the city than many of its citizens could claim. She had been sad to see him head back west with his FDG buddies, so finding him here was certainly a pleasant surprise.

Garcia saw them come toward him. He let the weight rack settle back to the stack. He looked to have been bench-pressing well over three hundred pounds, and Valerie gave him a nod of respect.

"Valerie!" he called, giving her a broad smile.

"Trying to bulk up in case there're hotties in space?" Valerie asked. "You know, I'm going to have to ask the colonel about how he feels about you hitting on the aliens…"

"You want to talk to me about love lives?" he laughed, then shared an awkward silence with the two.

"Yeah…" Robin pursed her lips, giving Valerie a curious glance before looking back at the sergeant. "Whatever you're trying to insinuate there, that's over. This is strictly business."

Valerie nodded. "Kill aliens. Save the world. And what-ever the hell that means."

Garcia chuckled. "Shi-it. I can tell you this much…I'm feeling that much safer knowing you two are on the job."

"I can say the same about you and your massive pecs,"

Valerie replied. "Just…I'm surprised to see you here. Earth couldn't handle any more Sergeant Garcia?"

"I thought the colonel was mad at me for being gone so long," he admitted. "Turns out, your pal Sandra had told him about me and he was impressed. So I got on the destroyer with the rest of the FDG in San Fran. Two platoons' worth."

"I can't think of any other non-mods that would deserve it more than you."

"Don't you start assigning labels like that. Up here, we're all soldiers of the Etheric Federation, am I right?"

Valerie nodded and Robin replied, "Damn straight."

"I'm sorry we didn't get more of a chance to chat back on Earth, by the way," Garcia said, offering his hand to Robin, which she accepted and shook with a firm grip that made him wince. "But I can see we're going to get along just fine."

"As long as you can spot me when I bench three times what you were just doing, we're good." Robin tried not to smile, which was fun coming from her.

"No need to start the pissing contest just yet, ladies," Valerie noted with a chuckle.

"I was just killing time, actually," Garcia said, winking at Robin. Valerie winced. Was he hitting on the girl?

"There's a big party you're waiting on?" Valerie asked.

Garcia shook his head, then motioned toward the others in the room. "Mods. Get this, we get a chip so we can chat with the ship's EI. Everyone."

"Fuck that," Valerie said. "I'm not putting a chip in me, and I definitely am not letting some EI get into my head."

He scoffed. "Yeah, have words with BA over that and

see how far that conversation takes you." He must've noticed her go pale, because he laughed. "I thought not."

Garcia waved Tyson Kurtz to him. "Lieutenant, these are a couple of the vamps I fought with over in New York." He pointed to one then the other. "Valerie and Robin."

"Nice to meet you. I'm Kurtz. We've been working with the colonels and their tac teams for a while now." He looked around the room and his eyes came to rest on three others who were fighting over a piece of workout equipment. "Hey, you stupid fuckers, come here! The big one is Edwin. Then Samantha, and finally our tech guru, Nick Rixon. I think Nick is a little behind the power curve when it comes to modern technology, because what we used to think was modern? It ain't."

"I'll second that," Nick admitted. The group shook hands.

"Hey, in our world, technology means you have a wine opener that isn't your teeth," Valerie stated with a laugh, noting how Nick failed to think that was funny.

"And your specialties?" the man asked.

Robin and Valerie glanced at each other, frowning.

"Um, killing?" Robin offered in response.

"Sounds about right." With a shrug, Valerie added, "That's what Earth demanded of us. It seems like it's what BA will require of us too."

"Yeah, but you two were something special back there, right?" Nick asked. "I mean, up here...being a Vampire is cool and all, but after the mods, it's not really a thing. Or, not in the same way it was, right? And here you're not just killing Weres, Foresaken, or...what did I hear you call it? Non-mods?"

"I get it," Valerie replied. "Bigger, badder enemies. I'm not so special." She glared, until Robin cleared her throat. "Mister Technonuts over here and I are going to get along just great, I can tell."

"More women is a plus as far as I'm concerned," Samantha interjected, clearing the tension. "Hell, the testosterone in this room alone is enough. Girl power."

Valerie nodded, then turned back to Kurtz. "I just realized, I have no idea how this is going to work. I mean, are we all on a team, part of some intergalactic strike force or something?

Kurtz shrugged. "That's a question higher-ups than me will have to answer. Likely the colonel or BA."

"And Michael? How's he play into all this?"

With a shake of his head, Kurtz answered, "Again, we'll see soon enough."

She wasn't sure how she felt about it yet, but she felt the agitation starting to get to her. She was up here because of Michael, yet he was off doing something else. How did that make sense? Maybe he meant to give her a role like back on Earth, when he had appointed her as his Justice Enforcer.

"I'd like to know too, honestly," Robin stated. "I left a lot behind, and want to be sure I did it to make a difference."

"You want action?" Kurtz asked. "You can count on that."

"Then what's the holdup?" Robin asked. "I don't get why we're being made to wait around."

Valerie shot her a reproachful glance, but she looked back to the others, just as curious as her friend.

Garcia pointed to the schedule displayed on a screen by the door. Valerie and Robin moved closer.

"They've got us on here," Valerie said flatly.

"We're all on there. No chance to get off the ship now, but we're going to space, another galaxy! That is the shit!" Garcia looked into the distance, lost in thoughts of the unknown and the fantastic.

Joseph stepped from the Pod Doc and breathed deeply, as if waking from a long slumber. He stretched and smiled.

Hugely.

"Petricia next," he declared before picking her up and swinging her around. The fact that Joseph was naked didn't bother anyone in the group. Weres were considered to be the beautiful people. They showed off without showing off. They didn't care about being naked or being around other naked people.

The children had grown up in that atmosphere. They ignored it, but they didn't go out of their way to take off their clothes in front of the others. They'd seen everyone as nature intended.

The technician looked away, but stole a glance at Petricia as she quickly removed her clothes and climbed into the Pod Doc. The door closed behind her.

"Well?" Ted was the first to ask the question. He stood close to Joseph, studying his features.

Joseph looked him up and down before shaking his head and turning to the others. He grinned as he spoke.

"Smedley has shared with me that I can now go into the

sunlight without being covered up, that I will no longer have to fight the urge to drink fresh blood." Joseph looked at the ceiling and cried out, "Thank you!"

He smirked at the group. "I need a new wardrobe, and she does, too."

Kaeden pointed to the FDG uniform, black fatigues. He pirouetted for the watchers.

"I was thinking maybe it's time to get away from black…"

"You wouldn't look good in rainbows," Marcie said. "Black uniform for you."

Joseph looked at her sharply from under a furled brow.

"I used to be somebody," Joseph said in a slight English accent with a wry smile.

"We all used to be somebody, but after seeing this?" Marcie waved her arms to take in the entirety of the spaceship. "We are all a bunch of nobodies doing what we can to stay on the Empress' good side."

Joseph clicked his tongue. "I'll accept that explanation, Mistress Marcie." He bowed to her. She rolled her eyes at him. Marcie had never understood some of the language he used, but he'd been born and raised in Europe well before the American Revolution.

He was the oldest of them all, only because Terry Henry had believed in him and given him a chance. Otherwise, he would have been yet another Forsaken, dead and withered under the pack's feet.

Joseph was young compared to the original Vampire, Michael, who was a great-great-grandfather of sorts. Even the Empress had given him a pass and now a gift. He took a knee and bowed his head, mumbling an oath of loyalty from far in his past.

The others watched him. When he stood, his dark eyes glistened. "I can't wait to get started. It's a whole new universe out there."

"Next!" the technician called as Petricia yawned and stretched, her nakedness on full display.

The man shook his head. He would never understand. He had set up a privacy curtain, but none of them were using it.

Marcie started to strip, but Ted ripped off his clothes at Werewolf speed and jumped in front of her. Felicity put a comforting hand on Marcie's shoulder. "I wish he was that excited about climbing in bed with me," she drawled quietly.

Marcie chuckled. "It's the ship, clearly. It's making everyone weird."

"I'm liking weird," Petricia declared, her arms still wrapped around Joseph's neck.

The technician turned back to the computers and watched the data stream as the Pod Doc took a sample, analyzed it, reprogrammed the nanos, issued new instructions, and injected additional nanocytes. The initial process took a total of thirty seconds. The rest of the time was dedicated to letting the body grow accustomed to the new equipment coursing throughout, subtly changing things, modifying and adding.

Ted was quick. Less than five minutes later, he stepped out and Marcie went in. He turned to the side and his eyes unfocused as he started a conversation with the ship's EI.

Felicity shook her head. "You know," she started in a

loud voice. "I had to coerce him to marry me. Three kids and a lifetime later, he's still Ted."

"No, Mom. He's not. I remember the old Ted. Distant, living in his own world, hiding within his mind. He still does that, sure, but he does so much more now. You've changed him a lot and for the better," Marcie told her. Marcie was already grown and married with her own children when Ted came into Felicity's life.

Before then, he'd been Uncle Ted, because that was what her closest friends Kim, Kae, and Cory had called him.

Ted loved technology. A nuclear engineer in the before times, he restored power to much of the world and then he built the gravitic engines, based on Kurtherian technology, that powered the fleets of dirigibles that plied Earth's skies. Ted's engines had made him and Felicity fabulously wealthy. She enjoyed it, not the money but the pampering that came with it.

Even that grew old, over time.

But the *War Axe* and a journey to a new galaxy as new people with a new mission. That was something they could all sink their teeth into. The destroyer represented hope, despite its ominous title.

Everyone could use a little hope.

The Pod Doc finished cycling and the door opened. Marcie stepped out, a shocked expression on her face.

Terry and Char followed Dokken to the mess deck, a large space with long tables for the passengers and crew to eat together as smaller groups. It was an inefficient use of space to feed the crew at one time. They were between lunch and dinner, yet half the seats were filled. Dokken stayed close to the wall, rounding the corner and following a second wall to an open area where food could be passed from the kitchen.

The German Shepard stopped and waited. He looked at the window and his tail wagged. Terry and Char caught up with him and peeked through. A young woman was there staring at Dokken.

She finally spoke. "I have no idea what a beef is? What? Who?" Terry waved apologetically.

"We brought some on board in San Francisco. It was frozen."

"That stuff? Do you know how to cook it?" the woman asked.

The smile started slowly, spreading across his face. Char nodded. "I do," he said simply.

The woman waved him and Char around back.

Smedley, can you summon the two platoons from the rec room? I could use some help and we have a few people who can butcher and cook far better than me. Maybe Auburn is done with what he needed to do?

>>I will contact them on your behalf. Is this an emergency?<<

I want to say yes, but the right answer is 'no.'

>>Aye, aye, Colonel,<< the EI replied.

Terry seemed to swell. "We have a plan. A little food prep team building. What do you think, Dokken?"

I think I'm hungry.

"Me, too, but it'll be a while. It will be well worth the wait, my furry friend."

The line cook led them through the kitchen and into a storage area that butted up against the outer hull of the great ship. He could see the double bulkheads where the stores and supplies could act as a buffer in case of a weapon strike.

The cases of beef were stacked neatly near the end. Terry wanted to have plenty, so he pulled two cases weighing a total of one hundred pounds. Char took one from him and together, they returned to the kitchen.

A commotion from the dining area signaled the arrival of the FDG. Terry dumped his box on a prep table and leaned out through the window. "Back here!" he called.

The two platoons converged before Lieutenant Kurtz started barking orders, selecting people to work in the kitchen and then designating their roles. The cleanup crew was disappointed, until Kurtz told them that they were eating first.

Dokken stood next to the prep table, staring at TH and panting. Terry started trimming the first piece of beef, but the knife wasn't as sharp as he liked. He pulled his own trusty knife, the one that had been with him since the fall of civilization. He wiped it on a towel and returned to trimming the meat.

With a clean line, he quickly cut off the other strip of fat, leaving a generous amount of meat attached. He sliced that into four pieces. He put his silvered blade down and picked up one of the freshly trimmed pieces. He held it up as if Dokken was going to beg for it.

"I'm sorry, buddy, sometimes you act like a dog and I forget that you're sentient."

I am a dog. What's the holdup? Don't make me jump up on that table and take care of business myself. They don't like it when I get up there. He nodded toward the cook, who was eyeing him knowingly.

Terry handed down the piece. Dokken almost took his fingers off as he grabbed it.

More, the German Shepard said with his mouth hanging open and his tongue lolling.

TH quickly fed the dog the other three pieces.

"What do you think?"

I think more is in order, just to be certain.

"So it beats bistok?"

It may. The dog's lips peeled back in a dog smile.

"I told you. Let's leave these good people to their work. A feast is in order, and we'll be in the way."

I'll catch up, Dokken replied, never taking his eyes from the next warrior working his blade, butchering the afternoon's dinner.

>>Colonel Walton, please report to the briefing room behind the bridge.<<

That sounds like an official summons. Can I bring Charumati?

>>Yes, but no one else. This is a private conversation between the Empress and you.<<

Terry wondered how she'd gotten aboard the *War Axe* as she'd taken a shuttle to the *ArchAngel II* with Michael while the FDG was loading up. Terry didn't bother replying. He leaned his head through the window. "Come on, crack snacker, show us to the briefing room."

Busy, Dokken replied.

"Come!" Terry bellowed. By the last echo, every human was frozen in place, barely breathing, giving the colonel room to conduct his business.

Only because I *want to,* Dokken said before drooping his way from the kitchen, tail nearly dragging and ears sagging. Terry and Char led the way into the corridor where Dokken perked up and started trotting toward the nearest stairs up.

TH and Char couldn't shake the feeling that they were back on a naval vessel, and as deadly as water could be, the cold vacuum of space had even less mercy on its victims.

They followed Dokken up the stairs and through a maze of corridors until they reached a door that was labeled as the captain's conference room.

Dokken pointed at the door with his nose. Terry and Char stood outside. "My old Marine Corps days suggest I should pound on the hatch, but having met Bethany Anne, I suspect she simply wants us to go in."

The door suddenly slid aside and Akio stood there, one of his own at each shoulder.

CHAPTER SIX

"Terry-san. We've been expecting you." Akio stepped aside to usher them in. Dokken ran past and directly to Bethany Anne, earning himself a good head-petting and ear-scratching.

"Thank you, Akio-sama," Terry replied as he and Char walked into the room. The bitches departed, leaving Akio behind. He continued to stand while the rest sat.

"How do you like the ship?" BA asked.

"I would call it a Chariot of the Gods, and to quote Erich Van Daniken from his book of that title, *the time has come for us to admit our insignificance by making discoveries in the infinite unexplored cosmos. Only then shall we realize that we are nothing but ants in the vast state of the universe. And yet our future and our opportunities lie in the universe, where gods promised they would.*"

"More than you fucking know, TH. More than you can ever fucking know," BA told him. She casually reached down to rest her hand on Dokken's head. The dog smiled.

"You know that he has an arch enemy on this ship," Terry said conversationally.

She laughed and looked at Michael. The first Vampire shook his head. "His name is Wenceslaus. He's a stowaway, but the captain adopted him." Michael nodded toward a nondescript man who had been sitting at the table, unnoticed. Terry kicked himself for not making an introduction. Char chewed her lip.

They were passengers on his ship.

"I'm Terry Henry Walton," TH said, not able to reach across the table to shake the man's hand. "And this is Charumati."

"Captain Micky San Marino, but you can call me Micky," the man said pleasantly. He had a slight accent that Terry couldn't place. "The good king Wenceslaus and Dokken will forever be at odds. It is in their nature, and Michael is far too kind. Wenceslaus doesn't like anyone, not even the cooks who feed him. I have no idea how that little bastard gets in my quarters, but every night when I finally make it to my bunk, there's a big dent on my pillow with a pile of orange hair."

Bethany Anne's eyebrows went up as she blew out a breath. Everyone around the table fell silent.

"Soon, I'll be transferring back to the *ArchAngel II*. My people and I will be out of your hair so you can get on your way to gate to Yollin space."

Terry and Char waited. BA held up her hands as if expecting a question.

"What do you need us to do?" Char asked. Terry rubbed her leg under the table. She had beat him to the punch, and he was good with that. Her question was exactly as he was going to ask.

"It's not me who'll be asking. It's Nathan Lowell, he works for my dad, General Lance Reynolds, as his intelligence chief. Which, of course, has an active branch, if you get my drift." She looked as if she anticipated a guilty pleasure.

Terry smiled. "Nothing like covert direct action to get the blood pumping."

BA pursed her lips. Terry's smile disappeared.

"The intel weenies are doing their thing, but the Direct Action Branch relates more to your post-Marine Corps activities, isn't that right, ArchAngel?"

"Yes, it is," said a pleasant voice that seemed to surround them. Terry wasn't sure that BA hadn't spoken again. The voices sounded similar. "I am ready to patch communications through if you'd like. I have Nathan standing by."

"Let's see what that old dog has to say," BA replied.

"Hello! Take me to your leader!" a man's voice echoed across the room. "Is this fucking thing on? Hello? Hello? For fuck's sake, this is a waste of time. It's just a call across the galaxy. What do you want, a kidney? BA? Is that you dicking around? I swear..."

Terry and Char chuckled.

"You'll do what, Nathan, you fucking flea-ridden mongrel?" BA interrupted with a smile.

"There you are, BA! Shit. I thought I'd lost you." Nathan stopped talking.

"We're short on time, Nathan. We have Michael, Terry Henry Walton, Charumati, Akio, Captain San Marino, and Dokken. Make your pitch, say what you have to say."

Nathan didn't hesitate.

"I have a little company out here called the Bad Company and I'm told you are the right man to lead one of its elements."

"The right couple, Mister Lowell." BA laughed quietly at the title. "Char and I work side by side in all things."

"Sweet. I would have it no other way. The Bad Company is built to acquire intelligence for the Federation and works to promote the Federation's creed. If you accept the appointment I'm offering, you will be honor-bound to Empress Bethany Anne. You will fight for your brothers and sisters in the company. We run a lean operation to make sure that our profits, because we sell services and products, is self-sustaining. We handle intersystem exports and imports, along with military realignment. You would be in charge of the military branch."

Terry leaned forward in his seat. His elbows were on the table, and he stared at a point on the wall as he listened with rapt attention.

"Terry Henry and Charumati from planet Earth, do you willingly join Bad Company? Will you consider yourself honor-bound to Empress Bethany Anne and fight for your brothers and sisters in the company?"

Char looked at Terry. He looked back, but didn't see her. His mind was embroiled within his own thoughts. He pushed away from the table and stood, clasping his hands behind his back as he began to pace.

"Nathan. The offer is such an honor and you don't even know me. I expect Akio has vouched for me and has told you that I've been honor-bound since the day his pod descended through the Colorado skies. From that day until now, I've done the Empress' bidding as best as Akio, Char, and I could determine." Terry squinted into the room's soft lights. Those seated around the table waited patiently.

"From my first days in the Corps, I fought for my brothers in arms. From the first day I met Char, I fought to protect her, and she fought to protect me. Our family started with Char's pack, and grew with our kids and their families. All of them are our inner circle, people we trust with our lives, who trust us with theirs."

Terry looked for a glass of water, but there wasn't anything. He coughed once and cleared his throat. He smiled at Char, and she nodded to him.

"It would be our honor to stand between Nathan Lowell, the Bad Company, and their enemies. An attack on one of us is an attack on all. We would rather die than leave one of our own in peril. I speak for myself, Char, and every member of the Force de Guerre, when I tell you that you can count on us. On a personal note, I will do everything in my power to ensure that there's a metric fuck-ton of bad guys giving their lives for their cause and not a single one from the FDG, or should I say, the Bad Company. And you can call me TH."

"Well, TH, you can call me Nathan, and I expected no less from someone who comes so highly recommended. You're an old military man so let me give you your orders. The Bad Company's mission is to evaluate, approve, and execute paid missions in support of the Etheric Federation. One. the mission must pass the smell test, subjectively approved by at least two executive members of The Company. Two. Approved missions will be executed with the appropriate level of violence as determined by the on-site commander. Three. The price must be right. I'll have someone meet you when you reach Onyx Station. They'll have the RFIs for you--the requests for interdiction."

"Sounds good, Nathan. Thanks for bringing us on board."

"I've sent some other material to ArchAngel for you. She'll transfer it to the *War Axe*. Look through it and get yourself up to speed. I think someone said it'll be a month before you arrive, so you have plenty of time. Choose wisely. Lowell out."

The comm channel closed. Dokken's panting was the only sound in the conference room.

Terry finally realized he was standing. He mumbled an apology and sat back down, only to get back up when Bethany Anne and Michael stood.

"I didn't even get a chance to give Nathan shit about running out of Pepsi on the Prometheus. He's never going to live that one down, as long as I can get a word in edge-wise." She looked purposefully at TH.

Terry whistled as he casually looked away. The Empress started to laugh as she moved around the table, taking Char's hand and looking into her sparkling purple eyes. "Love that color, Char. You are one in a billion." BA turned to Michael. "How would I look with purple eyes?"

Michael scratched his chin. "This is one of those setup questions." He looked to Terry for support and saw the understanding in the man's face. Michael turned back to BA. "I can't imagine what would make you more beautiful than you are now, so I won't even try."

Terry nodded in approval of the Vampire's solution.

"So, you don't know? I guess I won't bother TOM with

it." BA started to leave and stopped. "How are the upgrades coming?"

Terry wasn't sure what she meant.

"The Pod Doc," she clarified.

"It worked for us. I'm not sure about the others. We'll head there straight from here to check in," Terry replied.

"I ordered an upgrade to your Vampires. They came over with us. I hope they don't mind because the alternative wasn't acceptable," Bethany Anne said cryptically before leaving the conference room with Michael by her side and Akio following closely behind.

Captain San Marino excused himself and left through the room's other door. When it opened, Terry and Char could see the ship's bridge. Screens showed a massive ship blocking out most of the stars.

The *ArchAngel II*.

The Empress and her party would be returning to it, and that was why they had to leave. Terry and Char had no idea where she was going from there. For the Bad Company, it didn't matter. They had their mission.

It dawned on TH as he looked past the flagship. "We're in space."

"Does that make us cosmonauts?" Char asked.

The door to the bridge closed. Dokken stood at the other door and pranced back and forth.

"Something like that. The Bad Company. It's almost as good as Space Warriors from Space, or maybe Space Marine Studs."

Char wasn't going to be left behind. "Women Warriors of the Cosmos."

"Man Warriors of Humanity's Spacemen." Terry tipped his chin up. "From space, doing manly things."

"The Rainbow Unicorns?" Char asked.

"Maybe we'll just stick with Bad Company," Terry conceded.

"I think that's best. What do you think, Dokken?" Char asked.

Let me out. I gotta pee, the dog replied.

Terry slapped the panel and the door opened.

"What's wrong?" Kaeden said, concern creasing his brow as he started to panic.

"I can't feel the Etheric," she said sadly. She sighed as she clamped her eyes shut. "It's gone."

The technician turned in his chair. "That's a temporary impact from the process. The new nanos have to interact with the old nanos until they all speak the same language. You won't lose anything you've had, you'll only gain from this process."

Marcie looked at the man and sighed again, this time with relief. She hurried to the man and hugged him. He tried to get away, but was too slow. Kae didn't look happy. His incredibly beautiful wife was hugging another man.

While standing in her birthday suit.

Kaeden took her clothes to her and worked his way in between the technician and his wife. "Maybe you can get dressed?" he asked politely. She strolled casually toward the privacy curtain with an extra swing of her hips. The technician was staring at his computer screens and talking to himself.

The man's face was beet red.

"Put your clothes on, woman," Kae whispered.

"Yes, sir, man," she whispered back.

"How did I get so lucky?" He smiled at her as he followed her behind the curtain.

"Hey!" Timmons yelled. "They're trying to be the first to do it in space!"

"Nooo!" the technician blurted. "No doing it in the lab!"

Kaeden and Marcie reappeared moments later, both dressed.

"That quick? You're not giving mankind a good name, my friend," Timmons suggested.

"Next!" the technician yelled.

Dokken disappeared down a side corridor. Terry and Char easily found their way to the Pod Doc. The ship seemed a challenge at first, but it was laid out logically. They figured that everyone would be able to find their way around before they hit their bunks for the first time.

The smell of grilling beef filled the passageways of the *War Axe*.

Terry stopped and savored the aroma. "Maybe we can stop by the mess deck first?" he asked.

"We can call them," Char suggested.

"One of the many reasons for my never-ending love." Terry hugged Char and nibbled her ear.

"Later," she promised.

Smedley, can you contact our people in the medical area?

>>You can contact them yourself, TH. Say their name and my system will connect you through their implants. <<

"How cool is that?" Terry replied aloud.

Marcie, are you there. Can you read me, over?

It'll take some getting used to, TH, you being in my head and all. Do you know what I'm thinking? Marcie replied.

No. Should I? Terry wondered.

No, you shouldn't and you don't want to either. How horrible would that be?

You'd have to ask Joseph about that. I think it's more of a burden than a benefit. But that's not why I called. How is everyone?

Joseph and Petricia are better than great. No blood craving and they are now official daywalkers, sunlight won't bother them. Everyone else is fine. Merrit is in there now and he's the last one. I lost my ability to see into the Etheric dimension, but the tech assures me that it is only temporary. I feel empty without it.

Terry clenched his jaw. Marcie was his protégé when it came to the FDG. She understood things better, was better able to tolerate the sacrifices a leader had to make, order people into combat, even if there was a chance they'd die. She didn't like it, but she could do it, based on the needs of the mission, the acceptable risk versus the probability of success.

Meet us on the mess deck when you're finished, because lunch, or is it dinner, smells like it's ready. I'll send the next bunch of victims from there. See you at chow.

Terry turned toward the mess deck, but Char stopped him, holding her hands up.

"Sorry, I always assume you can hear my conversations, even when it's only me talking with myself," he said softly. She had demonstrated over the past century a prescient-level of understanding to such a degree that TH was convinced she could read his mind. "The Forsaken are Forsaken no more."

CHAPTER SEVEN

The mess deck was a buzz of activity. TH felt like he'd been physically slapped when he stepped through the door because of the volume of noise. The cook was yelling from the kitchen.

He made a calming motion with his arms, but the noise level didn't change. "SHUT UP!" he bellowed. All heads turned toward him. A utensil clanked loudly against a tray. "Thank you. Next group to the Pod Doc. Get on your horses and go. You have two minutes to report."

A number of people got up, first among them were Sergeant Garcia, Valerie, and Robin. The Vampires didn't look happy as they walked past TH without saying a word.

"Valerie," Terry said softly. "We'll talk later today, you three. There are some great things ahead, and we're going to need the best that we have."

Valerie hesitated for a moment before nodding tersely and heading into the corridor.

"Yes, sir. I look forward to it," Sergeant Garcia replied

formally before following the two Vampires out. Three other warriors joined them with Kurtz in the lead.

"Take care, Kurtz," Terry told the man.

"You bet, Colonel. Someone has to show our hard-chargers how it works and that there's nothing to be afraid of. There is nothing to be afraid of, right?"

"Not as far as you know," Terry replied, punching the lieutenant in the shoulder. Terry and Char left Kurtz standing there as they walked toward the kitchen. People were starting to talk again, but in more hushed tones.

The cook continued to yell. Kurtz and his two charges left the mess deck on their way to the Pod Doc. Terry tiptoed to the window and peeked in. Two warriors were dancing around the grill where the remnants of the Weathers beef were getting seared. The cook was laughing all the while yelling at them to be careful.

The kitchen had already been cleaned up. Two warriors were at the cleanup station running the last of the dishes through an alien cleansing and sanitation system.

"Welcome to the future," Terry said softly.

"No shit," Char agreed. "It's the same, but completely different. Those stupid bastards who tried to destroy Earth. Could we have been to this point, as a species?"

"I'd like to think so. But as different as things are, human nature will always be the same, even if they're aliens. I guess it is truly universal, otherwise, why would the Bad Company need to exist?"

Char chuckled. "Job security, lover. We will always have job security."

"Because there's always someone out there who needs their ass kicked. In the immortal words of Marine Corps legend, Mad Dog Mattis, 'The first time you blow someone away is not an insignificant event. That said, there are some assholes in the world that just need to be shot.' Change *world* to *universe* and there we are."

Char nodded before pointing to the trays. "Lunch?"

"Unless they're calling it dinner." Terry looked toward the door as he held his tray. He stopped and looked at the two men working the grill. "Have you two eaten yet?"

"Not yet, sir, but Jenelope has promised us something special, so please, go ahead," one of the men said, turning back to the grill.

"You know I eat last," Terry told them as he headed toward the opening to the kitchen.

"You'll eat when I tell you to eat!" Jenelope roared, storming toward the serving line.

Terry flinched and leaned back. "My God, that voice! It's Mrs. Grimes!"

"You'll keep a civil tongue in your head. Take your food and go. You're holding up the line." She jutted her chin toward him.

Terry looked past Char. No one was waiting.

"Is there a limit to how much we can take?" Terry asked sheepishly.

"There's one rule here. If you take it, you eat it." She pulled a wooden spoon from her apron and shook it at TH.

"What the hell is up with the wooden spoon?" Terry blurted, jumping back.

"Sounds good, Jen, and thank you," Char said pleasantly, stepping past TH and loading her tray with beef, and a small portion of vegetables.

"You could learn some manners from this one," the new

Mrs. Grimes said, waving her spoon ominously in Terry's direction.

"Yes, ma'am," he said as he stretched an arm as far forward as he could to spear two steaks and drop them onto his tray. He filled the rest of the space with a sampling of everything else. Jen narrowed her eyes at him.

"Mother fuck!" he whispered as he walked away.

"Is that the same person we met earlier?" Terry asked as he sat down next to Char at the end of a long table. A number of warriors were sitting nearby chatting. Everyone was on hold as they waited for their turn in the Pod Doc. The schedule was filled for twelve hours straight before the process would be completed for all the new additions to the crew.

The hatch opened and Dokken trotted in.

"Yes, she's the same, but with this mob, she's had to put on her mom hat," Char explained.

"I see. I wonder how many arch enemies she has?" Terry dug into his steak and moaned in pleasure as he chewed. Char laughed, until she did the same thing.

They ate in silence until the pack arrived with Terry and Char's family in tow. Or it could have been the other way around. Marcie was in front, until she saw the chow line. She stood back to let the others pass. The Werewolves had no compunction about eating first. Sue and Timmons, Shonna and Merrit, led the way, followed by Felicity and Ted. The Vampires went next, leaning back and forth to get a better look at the meat tray as they neared.

Aaron walked with Yanmei. When she rounded the corner, they saw that she had an orange bundle in her arms. Terry's eyes shot wide. Instantly, Dokken unleashed a broadside of spittle-flecked barking. He'd been trolling the tables, getting hand-fed scraps of beef. He was in between tables and refused to be denied access to his quarry.

His arch enemy was in sight!

He leapt onto a table, landing among the trays and sending them flying as he launched himself toward the cat. He hit the deck, slid, and quivered at Yanmei's feet as he barked furiously.

Wenceslaus stretched out an orange paw to show his claws before yawning and resting his head on Yanmei's arm.

"SHUT UP!" came the yell from the kitchen, a mirror of TH's earlier call for silence. Jen stormed up the line and wielding her wooden spoon with deadly accuracy, smacked the enraged Dokken on top of his head.

The German Shepard yipped and jumped back. Terry hurried to join the group.

"What's he doing in here?" Terry demanded.

Yanmei looked behind her, wondering who Terry was talking about.

"Him?" Aaron asked, pointing.

"He's our arch enemy," Terry stated slowly, glaring at the cat.

"He's a cat, TH," Yanmei said softly.

Wenceslaus meowed.

"What did he say?" Terry leaned closer to the orange creature.

"How would we know? He's just a cat." Aaron said, stepping between Terry and Dokken and Yanmei. Aaron's unnatural height meant that Terry had to look up, but

Aaron was a gentle soul, despite being a Weretiger. He and his Weretiger wife were most at peace with the universe.

But Terry had convinced them that if someone had the ability to act, they had the responsibility. Aaron and Yanmei had exceptional gifts and they had used them to benefit all humanity.

If they wanted a cat as a pet, who cared.

Terry reached past Aaron toward the good king to pet his orange head, but the cat lashed out at nearly vampiric speed and raked three lines across the back of Terry's hand.

"Why you little bastard!" Terry looked at his hand, unconcerned with the scratch that was already healing. Kim, Kae, and Cory held up their hands. The slight white lines of scratches were there, but fading.

"Even you?" Terry asked Cordelia.

She used one finger to pull the hair back on the side of her head, exposing her ears. She was born to a Werewolf, but wasn't a Were. She had two features from her mother's true nature--a silver streak of hair and wolf ears.

Cory shrugged and rubbed the back of her hand. A faint blue glow appeared. When she removed her hand, there was no sign that there had ever been an injury.

"Have you sworn fealty to our arch enemy?" Terry asked, starting to smile. He reached down and scratched behind a confused Dokken's ears.

"He's a cat, TH. We swear nothing to this creature. He simply exists in our world," Yanmei explained.

Terry mumbled something unintelligible. "Come on, buddy, we have steak to eat. I have a nice big T-bone with your name on it."

Dokken barked one last time, dodged expertly beneath the wooden spoon, and chased after Terry Henry.

Terry exercised great restraint in not turning at the sound of a spoon impacting flesh. He was better off not knowing. Jenelope started yelling as she returned to the kitchen and feet again started shuffling past the serving area.

The door opened and Kurtz stepped out. He felt wildly different. A dull pain coursed across his shoulder blades. The technician looked at him in alarm. Kurtz immediately checked himself, patting his body with his hands. He flexed and his muscles bulged like never before. "Oh yeah." He smirked.

The warriors in the room watched him carefully, stepping back to give him space.

"What's wrong with you twat waffles?" he asked. One of them pointed to a mirror. He snarled at the young woman. When he reached the mirror, he froze. His shoulders were hunched in a way that looked unnatural, but to him, felt powerful. His eyes had a distinct yellow glint, his irises more canine like. "What the hell is wrong with me, doc?"

Kurtz threw his clothes on before stomping the few meters to get to the technician. His clothes fit more tightly than when he'd taken them off. The man looked terrified.

Alarm klaxons sounded in the corridor.

Lieutenant Kurtz felt trapped. "Are we under attack? Where the hell do we go? Where is our duty station?" He looked around frantically before bolting through the door and down the passageway.

The other warriors followed him, but the technician yelled at them to come back. "We have a schedule to keep," he said calmly, showing no trace of his earlier fear. He pointed to the young woman. "You next."

She pulled the privacy curtain in front of the Pod Doc, undressed, and got in. The door shut and the technician went about his work, surreptitiously watching a status locator in the upper corner of his screen. The new Werewolf was running through the corridors where he would find a security team waiting.

The technician feared the worst--that the man hadn't changed into just a Werewolf, but a Pricolici. They'd been experimenting, but not on live tissue. There had to have been something in Kurtz's DNA that made him susceptible.

He needed to be controlled until he could control himself.

"What?" Terry exclaimed. "Son of a bitch!"

Char's muscles tensed as she knew what was coming next. Terry jumped from his seat and started running for the door. "Tac teams with me. NOW!"

The pack hesitated for an instant, before Char's fierce look galvanized them into action. A cat raced across the tabletop in front of them, diving through the open door just behind Terry Henry.

Five Werewolves, two Weretigers, and the FDG senior officers raced out, single file, through the door and down the corridor after the colonel, having no idea where he was going or why.

And it didn't matter. He called for help and they went. Without question. Without remorse.

—

Kurtz wasn't sure where he was going, but thought the hangar deck the best candidate. Shuttle pods were located there. The teams would use them for a landing operation. He wondered if that meant a breaching operation, too. Kurtz had no idea what that looked like, but was ready to go kill someone.

He was angry, but didn't know why. His clothes started to split.

The blow came from nowhere. A strike hard enough to send him flying through the air and slamming into a steel bulkhead. He felt bones break when he hit. Pain shot through his limbs.

He slid down to the deck, landing in a crumpled heap.

"What the fuck is wrong with you?" Valerie asked. "You don't just change for no reason."

"Change?" he mumbled as he struggled upright to sit back against the bulkhead.

Robin approached from the side as Valerie kneeled in front of the lieutenant. "You don't know?"

Kurtz shook his head.

"I'm not going to be the one to tell you," she replied as she stood.

CHAPTER EIGHT

Terry Henry and his tac teams ran onto the hangar deck, turning and making a beeline for Valerie, Robin, and Garcia.

"TH," Valerie said as a greeting.

Terry decided if they were going to a new galaxy together, he needed all the friends he could get.

"What's going on?" he asked, tipping his head toward the man on the ground.

"Didn't want to rough him up," Valerie replied, "but he left me little choice."

Robin simply nodded, getting her girl's back.

Char worked her way around the others and took a knee next to Kurtz. Cory joined her. When he looked up, they saw everything they needed to see. The yellow eyes gave him away. Char leaned back, closed her eyes, and started to draw power from the Etheric dimension. She could sense the others, see how their bodies interacted with the Etheric connection.

And Kurtz was pulling more than anyone else. His body

was hungrily drawing the power. The Pod Doc had changed him.

"Back to sickbay with you," Char told him.

"What's wrong with me?" Kurtz asked in a sad voice.

"You're becoming a Were, not just any Werewolf, but a very rare kind, a *Pricolici*." Char was patient as the man's jaw worked against itself. He wrestled with the changes.

The unwanted changes.

"I didn't ask for this," he said as he struggled to his feet. Char and Cory helped. The others stepped back. Cory's touch calmed as it always did. She kept her hand on the back of his neck where the pain of his change found purchase.

"We'll see what we can do for you," Terry offered.

Smedley, stop all Pod-Doc work immediately until I am comfortable with what it's doing to my people. None of us need a ship full of rabid Werewolves.

>>The current process is ongoing with no issues,<< the EI replied.

When that one ends, no more until we find out what the hell happened to Kurtz.

Terry closed the link without waiting. They ushered Kurtz up the stairs, around corners, and down hallways until they returned to the room with the Pod Doc.

The last of the warriors was exiting. He hurriedly got dressed, while keeping a wary eye on Lieutenant Kurtz.

"How do you feel?" Terry demanded of the man.

"There's someone talking in my head, but outside of that, I feel fine, sir. Am I supposed to feel bad or something? The lieutenant looks like shit."

"I think he just had a reaction to it, that's all. Go to the chow hall and tell everyone to rally up in the rec room. I'll meet you all there in ten."

"Sir, yes, sir!" The private ran out. Marcie stopped the man.

"I'll take care of it, Colonel," Marcie shouted from the corridor. Terry mumbled his agreement while keeping his eyes on the lieutenant.

"He's going back in the Pod Doc," Terry said.

The technician stood and shook his head.

"What's your name, son?" Terry asked.

"They call me Bob," the man replied.

"Well, Bob, I need you to explain to me why this man has been turned into a FUCKING PRICOLICI!"

The man rocked back from the force of Terry's yell.

"I need you to calm down," the man said, looking down his nose at the colonel.

Terry dove forward, his hand outstretched as he reached for the man's throat. Char intercepted her husband with a full body block, driving him into the Pod Doc. They wrestled briefly, but Terry knew that Char was right.

He so loved wrestling with her. He smiled up at her sparkling purple eyes. He was on his back and she straddled him. She knew when the fight was out of him. She popped to her feet and pulled him up.

Bob was backed up against his console, still looking afraid.

"What's a Pricolici?" a weak voice asked.

"Pricolici are Werewolves, but they walk upright and are more violent. They can also speak while in Were form, while a Werewolf or a Weretiger cannot," Timmons stated clinically as if lecturing a student.

Terry looked to Char for confirmation. She shook her head.

"I've never met one before."

"It looks like maybe now you have," Terry answered before turning back to the technician. "What can you do to fix this, Bob?"

"There is nothing to fix. Those genes and nanocytes were already in his system. The Pod Doc only activated what lay dormant."

"How could he already have those genes? He had nothing to do with Weres before he met us. He's a good ol' country boy, joined the FDG and did good," Terry said.

"All of you have it to some extent," Bob explained. "But your active nanocytes are dominant. There were a few who we've checked who did not have the nanocytes. Let me see…" The technician scrolled through data on his screen. "Felicity and Auburn."

Terry looked into the corridor. "What makes you different from the rest of us?"

Cory gasped. "They are the only ones I haven't had to heal."

"We birthed Typhoid Mary?" Terry asked, half-joking. Char punched him in the chest hard enough to drive him backward.

"Dad might be right," Cory said barely above a whisper. Joseph put a comforting hand on her shoulder. "I'm sorry, Tyson, I didn't know."

Kurtz smiled at her. "How can I be angry with you? All

you've ever done is try to heal the world. It's not in your nature to hurt someone, not knowingly."

"This is him as he really is," Bob told them.

"Bullshit," Terry replied coldly. "None of these people had any of this stuff before. Run your analysis by cross-checking the nanocyte interactions starting with Char and me, then add in the information you have on Akio, and finally, look at Cory's. Don't look at her data in isolation."

"Damn, TH," Timmons replied. "I've never heard you sound like a scientist before."

"Too much TV during my formative years," Terry replied, watching Bob's eyes brighten as if a lightbulb turned on within his mind. The technician hurried to his seat, mumbling about not knowing the cross-pollination of the nanocytes since he'd never heard of such a thing before. Using nanos to heal people, yes, but not that they would integrate with existing nanocytes.

"All that research time, but here it is, what we've been looking for," Bob said.

"What?" Terry asked, leaning over the man's shoulder and looking at a screen filled with incomprehensible data.

Marcie walked through the door to the mess deck, turned right, and headed around the tables to the serving window. "Cleaning party," she called, but not in a loud voice.

Two warriors hurried to her side.

"Are we cleaned up and ready to go?" she asked.

"Yes, ma'am," one of them said.

Marcie walked into the kitchen, head held high. "Jenelope! Master chef! Are you in here?"

"Who's in my kitchen?" she replied from a back corner.

"Colonel Marcie Walton, ma'am. I want to make sure that you are satisfied that my people properly cleaned this space for you following our impromptu meal."

Jen wiped her hands on her apron as she approached. She looked to the sides and motioned conspiratorially for Marcie to lean closer. Jen moved close to the colonel's ear before whispering. "The space actually cleans itself. There are a couple bots that take care of it, but I let your people do it, because they said they had to, following orders and stuff. You'll find that this ship takes care of most of the little things so its crew can take care of the big things."

Marcie tried not to chuckle. She leaned around the side of Jen's head. "That can be our little secret. If we don't have them clean up after themselves here, they'll think that there will always be someone to make their beds for them. If you're okay maintaining the charade, I'll assign daily work parties for each meal."

"I appreciate the company, Marcie," Jen said in a normal tone. "My, aren't you pretty. Are you what's left of humanity on Earth?"

Marcie smiled at the compliment, having not realized that the crew may not have been informed of the mission or the newcomers.

"No. We are only a tiny fraction. Humanity is thriving again, and I'd like to think that my in-laws had a lot to do with that. Bethany Anne has given us a different mission. We're going to the stars, join Nathan Lowell's Bad Company, and the *War Axe* is taking us."

"I wondered," the woman replied, looking forlornly at the warriors gathered around the tables in the dining area. "Will some of them die?"

Marcie hadn't expected the conversation to turn dark. She knew the universe had to be a wonderful but dangerous place and couldn't wait to get out there and see it for herself.

"Not if I can help it," Marcie promised, gripping the cook's shoulder, before turning and facing the dining area. "And that means training! To the rec room, people. We've had a change in schedule."

The warriors filed out in a hurry, leaving a couple members of the crew sitting by themselves. Marcie wondered when they'd be able to get to know the crew.

She wondered about the classes, too, and realized that the amount of information she didn't know about the things that would directly impact her life far outweighed what she did know. Marcie had never felt so helpless before. She gritted her teeth and shook off the feeling.

When you're in a strange place, do something that you know.

Marcie knew sparring. Hand-to-hand combat training would put everyone at ease, while making them sharper, and buying time for Terry Henry and Char to figure out what happened to Kurtz.

***

"Enhanced Vampire nanos have integrated with the enhanced Werewolf nanos," the technician said slowly as he pointed at various cells within the complex dataset displayed on his screen. "Terry and Char's nanocytes are supercharged. Akio's nanos are greatly enhanced. Cory received everything that her parents have, but tempered. If she wants to become a Werewolf, there's only one slight mod we need to make."

Bob studied his screen momentarily before continuing.

"When Cory healed Akio, and his nanos merged with hers, that is when the Pricolici strain was born. The four of you have created an independent series of nanocytes that have taken on a life of their own. To the system, they look like recessive traits, dormant until activated."

"Cory has healed a lot of our people," Terry said matter-of-factly. "We're in a dangerous business and have a tendency to get injured maybe a little more often than other people."

"How do we make sure that none of the others are turned into something they don't want to be?" Char asked.

"We know what to look for. ArchAngel's program will be able to restrain further excursions into the realm of the Pricolici. We will simply insert a chip and improve the healing capabilities of your people as a first step or as an only step, whatever you need. You are in charge of these conversions." Bob leaned back in his chair and threw his hands behind his head.

"How are you feeling, Kurtz?" Terry asked.

"Getting better by the minute, sir. I think I like it, but I'm going to have to ease into it. Kind of came as an unhappy surprise."

"I'll help you to understand," Char told him. "The most important thing you can do right now is stay calm. If you change when you aren't ready, the consequences could be dire."

"I tell him to stay calm, and he tries to wring my neck. You tell that one to stay calm, and everyone's like, 'oh yeah. That's right.'" Bob's lip curled.

Terry clenched his fists, making his knuckles turn white. "Bob. I think it best if you don't talk."

Kaeden squeezed in next to the technician. "I'd listen to him if I were you."

"You need me more than I need you!" the man blurted before clasping a hand over his mouth.

Kae grabbed the man by the back of his collar and dragged him from the room. "We're going to have a little chat, Bob," Kae told him as he propelled him down the corridor.

Shonna slid easily into the seat, cracked her knuckles, and tapped on the screen. "Smedley, you're going to teach me how to use this thing."

"This is most irregular," the EI replied. "Maybe if Ted asked, we could start at a higher level."

Shonna's expression turned sour. "Then tell Ted to get his ass down here," Shonna sneered.

"Done."

Silence filled the room. Terry and Char took that as their cue to leave. "Keep me informed," Terry said over his shoulder.

Timmons worked his way close to the monitors and studied the screens. He shook his head. "I got nothing."

"Me either," Shonna replied. "I know that Smedley is right, but it chaps my ass when he has to say it out loud in front of everyone else.

Ted walked in less than thirty seconds after being summoned. He looked at Shonna in front of the monitors and stopped in confusion.

"We need you to run this thing," Shonna said flatly.

"What happened to the technician?"

"Bob was a raging, flaming asshole and got on the wrong side of TH. He's not welcome to work with our people."

"But this isn't our ship, and this isn't our equipment," Ted stammered, frozen in place.

"We're sharing. Smedley said he would let only you work the controls. He didn't want to go back to two-plus-two level for us Neanderthals."

"He got that right," Ted said.

Shonna balled a fist. "Sometimes, Ted, I just want to beat the crap out of you."

"Don't make me sic Felicity on you," Ted countered.

Shonna stood and offered the chair, eyes narrowed in thought. "If I didn't know you better, I would think that you just made a joke. I take it back. You earned yourself a reprieve." She dragged a hand across his back and he cringed.

Ted didn't like to be touched, but he'd gotten better over the centuries.

As soon as the Werewolf genius dug into the data, everything and everyone else disappeared to him. He started talking out loud. The group knew that Smedley was instructing him through Ted's chip. Then the EI switched to the speakers. They talked simultaneously. The screens flashed as Ted's hands flew across them.

No one could follow what was happening, so they left.

"Tell us when you're ready for the next victim," Timmons told the back of Ted's head as the tactical teams meandered in the general direction of the recreation room.

Edwin, Samantha, and Nick stood in the center of the ring. "Fuck you candy-asses!" Edwin yelled. The three of them had trained and deployed with the tactical teams led by the Were and the enhanced. They'd been driven to the edge of natural human abilities.

Sometimes over the edge and Cory had to help them back to their feet. All of them had gotten time in Akio's cobbled-together Pod Doc back on Earth, in the time before Bethany Anne's return. They were in the best shape of all the warriors. They were the deadliest natural humans, because Terry Henry had demanded it.

Terry and the tactical teams only fought others from the UnknownWorld. Natural humans would readily die against them, unless they were trained to the degree of these three.

And Kurtz, but he was now one of them. He wouldn't spar again until he could control his power.

"Come one, come all. Your next beat-down awaits!" Edwin bellowed.

CHAPTER NINE

A warrior of similar size, a relative giant of a man strolled into the ring. "I'll bite," the man said in a deep baritone. They'd sparred before and Edwin had always handed the other man his ass. But it had been awhile and they'd both kept in shape. Maybe the contender had learned some new tricks.

The warriors lined the outside of the ad hoc ring and shouted encouragement. The two big men squared off. They bowed to each other as Terry Henry Walton had taught them to do.

Always respect your opponent.

They started to circle, neither crossing their feet as they kept their arms wide, using more of a wrestler's approach than anything else. Edwin darted in, dipped, dodged, and tried a reverse leg sweep. The opponent kicked the approaching leg and stopped it cold, then dove forward to deliver an atomic flying elbow.

Edwin rolled out of the way and back-flipped to his feet, then charged in.

The big man rolled to his back to catch the incoming and expected blow, but Edwin twisted sideways and back-kicked the man in the top of the head. He followed with an overhead chop, hammering the man's exposed nose.

Blood shot to the sides. But the big man was hardly finished. He rolled up, kicking his feet over his head and catching Edwin in the middle of a second pile-driver. The toes of two boots caught Edwin in the chest and threw him into the spectators.

The big man rolled sideways and came to his feet. Blood streamed down his face. Edwin shook off the heavy blows he'd taken and waded forward, fists up and ready.

The forward kick came too slowly. Edwin twisted just far enough to avoid the impact. He grabbed the man's leg and swung an uppercut into his groin. He lifted the big man and turned, driving him headfirst into the thin mat.

"Enough!" Colonel Marcie Walton ordered. Edwin took a knee next to the big man to see if he was conscious. "Maybe next time," the warrior told him. Edwin helped him to his feet and the crowd cheered.

<hr>

Valerie leaned against the wall, arms crossed as she watched the shenanigans. Back home in New York, they had never put on shows like this, or really bothered to fully test each other. There was martial arts training and some grappling, but it was always about making sure everyone was in tip-top shape, ready to take on the challenges of the world outside the city's walls.

They hadn't wanted to hurt each other, and even more

so once the violence was over. Hell, at that point everyone wanted to see as little action as possible. Everyone, but her and Robin. They wanted to get out there and save the universe, and here they were.

Of course, back then there wasn't the amazing healing pod that this ship apparently had. And she supposed that going up against aliens was an entirely new affair, one that pushed them to new levels of preparedness.

"Ladies, ladies, ladies," Garcia said, walking over to stand in front of them, eyes narrowed mischievously. "I think we all know it's your turn."

"You want me to fight," Robin leaned in, smiling to show her Vampire teeth, "it'll be to the death."

"Not here," he countered.

"Then we best not," she replied flatly.

Valerie simply watched the two with a smile. Garcia was a tough nut, but him against Robin? Yeah, right. She'd quickly earn herself the title of "The Nutcracker."

He considered this for a moment, eyes darting back and forth to each of them. "Maybe the two of you could put on a demo. Give the others something to aspire to?"

Robin shrugged, her eyes moving to Valerie curiously.

"What the hell, it'll kill twenty seconds," Valerie said. "But..." She lowered her voice as she addressed Robin, "...are you sure you can handle this?"

"Let's see what you got, old lady," Robin shot back with a mischievous smile.

"Old...lady?" Valerie stood, shaking her head. "You're in for a world of pain, little one."

The warriors cleared the ring and lined the space, giving the Vampires room.

Valerie circled her friend, this young woman who had been so much more to her, as they squared off. Not used to fighting for fun or show, Valerie had to pull back the first punch as she lunged forward.

Robin caught it and countered with a knee, holding her tight as she said, "Quit the bullshit. No holding back," before shoving her away.

Valerie rubbed her side where the knee had hit, watching Robin circle around her like a lion ready to pounce. Okay, that was how it was going to be?

This time, Robin came in, but pulled back at the last minute in a feint. Valerie over-committed and Robin came in with a leg sweep that caught her off-guard but didn't trip her.

Right—the woman had been trained as an assassin, of course she was going to use trickery and not simply come in swinging. Not her typical opponent.

This time, Valerie decided to be tricky too. As Robin recovered, Valerie came in with a leap to her left, but just as quickly pushed off and came around to the right, bringing her leg up for a roundhouse kick to Robin's ribs that sent her flying onto her back.

"Holy balls," Robin said, pushing herself up and turning to stretch her neck with a crack. At first, Valerie wondered if she'd gone too far, but then the younger woman smiled and added, "That's what the fuck I'm talking about!"

Valerie was caught off-guard by her friend swearing, but she guessed that was how she knew this was for real. The woman rarely went there, but now she was on the balls of her feet, moving around Valerie with hands held up, one slightly in front of the other.

"You sure you're ready for this?" Valerie asked with a cautious glance around at the others watching.

"Don't kill each other," Garcia called out, earning him a bit of nervous laughter from the others.

"Just a bit of fun," Robin countered, and had that same look in her eyes she used to get right before Valerie went in for a kiss. Was she getting a tad *too* much into this? It almost made Valerie laugh, but when Robin had suddenly come in with a reverse elbow that caught her on the lip and drew blood, followed by an uppercut and push-kick that sent her stumbling back, it wasn't so funny.

Valerie recovered from the moment of shock and caught the roundhouse kick, throwing Robin back over herself. When the younger woman landed on one knee, Valerie was there to catch her with a kick to the side of the head, instantly straddling her and putting her into a leglock.

"Tap out!" Valerie shouted, but Robin was just laughing like a crazy person.

"You gotta do better than that to tap this," she said, pushing through the pain as she called Valerie's bluff and pulled free from the hold.

As much as Valerie was getting into this, she wasn't about to break her friend's leg.

They both sprang into action, moving around each other on the ground and taking one hold after another, each breaking out to deliver blows before the next hold, but neither willing to break the other's limbs or even snap tendons.

When Robin took Valerie in a triangle hold and hit her twice in the face, Valerie pulled her into the air and slammed her onto her back, breaking the hold and knocking the wind out of her.

She was about to leap onto her with a downward elbow, when Garcia shouted, "Whoa, whoa."

He stepped forward, waving his hands. "Ladies, I think that's enough. Okay? Okay?!"

Valerie stumbled back, caught off-guard and realizing she had been too close to losing herself in the fight. A glance around showed nervous expressions.

"I...I wasn't going to really hurt her."

Robin pushed herself up to sitting, a look of confusion on her face that Valerie imagined matched her own. "It was just some fun, guys. No biggie."

Colonel Marcie Walton nodded toward Garcia, then stepped forward and helped Robin up. "Whatever you two want to call that, it's enough. Great demonstration, ladies. We all now know that you can kick some major ass, and that you have a little tension built up between the two of you."

Chuckles from around the room.

"Had," Robin countered, winking at Valerie. "Am I right?"

Valerie nodded, horrified at the blood trickling down Robin's brow where she must've busted it at some point. It would heal soon enough, but it suddenly hit her that she had caused the younger woman to bleed. Not her finest hour.

"Had," Valerie agreed. "Past tense." As she reached out to shake Robin's hand, she added, "Good fucking fight. I mean it."

"Right back at you. Though I still say you took it easy on me."

Valerie smiled and found a place away from the others where she could lean against the wall. Right now, she just wanted to be alone to clear her head from this mess. Maybe she had gone easy on her, maybe she'd lost control. It was a bit of both, and neither made her proud at that moment. Not that the actions were wrong, but that neither had been from a point of strategy. Rather, she'd been reacting to her emotions, letting them take over. She would have to learn how to control that.

"Whoa! Did you see that shit?" Nick Rixon shouted. "That was the bomb!"

"Come on, Colonel Walton. You got skills. Pair off and show us," somebody yelled.

Marcie strolled into the ring and the warriors started to cheer her on. Garcia felt bad because the cheers were so one-sided. No one knew who Valerie or Robin were. Garcia had been on detached duty with them for nearly a year. He returned right before the *War Axe* picked them up.

He'd been too busy to tell anyone about the Vampires.

She held her hands up, but the warriors continued to yell. "QUIET!" She stared down the group, turning slowly.

"Do you know who this is?" Marcie asked. Most shrugged.

"Valerie and Robin. They're like Akio, but they're new to the FDG. Have any of you besides Garcia made them feel welcome?" The warriors wouldn't meet her gaze.

She took a deep breath, put one hand in a pocket, and used the other to make an expansive sweep. "Terry Henry Walton started the Force de Guerre one hundred and thirty years ago to deal with a gang of raiders who were threatening New Boulder. Terry, Char, and four warriors rode out on horseback to take the fight to the enemy, better to fight them away from what the FDG was trying to protect. Sawyer Browne was killed and Char took the pistols she carries to this day from his dead body. Many of those in Sawyer Browne's band were rescued and brought into the fold."

Part of FDG training included the history. All the warriors had heard it before, except for the two Vampires.

"Since that day, Colonel Walton has been the moral compass that we follow. Honor. Courage. Commitment. Saying those words doesn't matter. It's living up to them that we strive for, every single day. Do you do the right thing when no one is watching? Only you can answer that, but we would like to think so. We'd also like to think that you'll do anything for your brothers-in-arms. That includes Valerie and Robin. Now make them feel welcome, bitches! And then run through level three Marine Martial Arts, first-degree black belt techniques. Fitzroy, lead them."

Marcie looked at the group as they formed rough lines within the confined space. Corporal Fitzroy was a stout woman with a mean bark. She took her position in front and started issuing commands. Marcie looked at Valerie and pointed toward the door.

Without looking back, Colonel Marcie Walton walked into the corridor. She took a few steps and stopped, waiting until she heard the other two and the door to close.

"Welcome to the FDG," Marcie said. "For the record, I'm not a big fan of lone wolves. I wasn't raised around any and for good reason--the loners never survived. We made it because of teamwork. Fought some bad-asses and we fought some candy-asses who had big guns. We've lost people, good people, a Vampire, Werewolves, and too many warriors. We almost lost Akio, too. No matter how big and bad you are, there's always someone who can bring more. It grates on my soul to be vulnerable in this ship because space is the great equalizer."

Marcie smiled and chuckled. Valerie and Robin watched her, emotionlessly, without responding.

"I'm not challenging you and I don't want to fight, but we will spar. We all need to improve. And it'll help pass the time as we travel to parts unknown. Well, unknown to us anyway. I want you to be a part of the team, but I don't know what that looks like. Help me understand how to make this work for you," Marcie said in her most tactful voice.

Valerie chewed on the inside of her lip before answering. "I came up here for a reason, and that's to kick ass and do my part to save humanity. You want me to train so I'm a better part of the team? I'll do it. You all want me to play friendly and maybe even teach some of the others up here a thing or two? I'm your gal." She took a breath, considering how much she should spill. Whatever, she decided. "And Michael invited me, so I assume he had something in mind. Something other than…sparring."

"We all have a greater purpose, but we all spar. We all train. The time will come and I'm sure we'll all get the action we're looking for."

"Wonderful. I'm just saying that I had friends, a family in a way. So did Robin. We left them behind for that action, so the sooner the better."

Marcie looked at the two Vampires, unsure of their commitment to the team. She knew that she'd have to talk with TH about how to handle them.

"Everyone has to start somewhere. Or start over. I was married with two kids when I finally decided to take the plunge. I did it on a whim because my husband said he had to join. We're not in a male-dominated society anymore. Why did I have to stay with the kids?"

"But you answer to TH, and he's a man," Valerie said softly.

"He's in charge because he's earned the right to be in charge, not because of differences in chromosomes, but he promoted me to an equal rank. For fifty years, I led the FDG. He's the right one to be in charge. He saved Earth," Marcie said proudly.

"There were a lot of people fighting to save Earth," Robin interjected.

"I'm sure. But Terry was fighting to save it for everyone else. He preferred not to fight, but to win the people over. If someone gave me shit, I'd punch them in the face. Easy day. Not TH. He fought as a last resort and that is what makes him great. He wins people over, makes people want to do what he asks. And when the bad guys call down the thunder, well, that's what they get. I watched the colonel jump three stories into a pack of Weretigers because they were threatening his wife. He killed them all. He killed a Vampire with his bare hands, after being tortured. That Forsaken was a powerful one that could read minds.

Never underestimate the colonel. I've heard that you're as fast as Akio. That's all well and good, but we still win as a team."

Marcie pinched her lips together as the two Vampires watched her. Neither attempted to reply. Marcie nodded once and headed toward the stairs. She wanted to check on the status of the Pod Doc, maybe talk with Terry Henry and Char.

Marcie took one step and heard the furious barking of the German Shepard.

Kurtz sat on his bunk, holding his head in his hands. Terry and Char leaned against the opposite wall, holding hands and unsure of what to do.

They were in the small room that had been assigned as the lieutenant's quarters. They watched the fledgling Were struggle with the emotions simmering within. He wanted to unleash his fury, but he was a well-trained warrior, disciplined. He wanted to explore the boundaries of his new powers.

"I feel like a volcano that's ready to blow. Does that ever go away?"

Char leaned forward. "It gets easier to control over time. You change form when you want to, not when the Werewolf takes charge. You can never let the Were run free. The more you do, the easier it will be to lose yourself. If that happens, the animal has taken over and you'll never be able to change back into human form. If that happens, you'll be hunted down and killed because you'll be a threat to humanity. Change on your terms and never, ever let the beast run free."

Kurtz threw his legs on his bunk and laid back. He draped an arm over his face to block out the light.

"Is it always this bright?" he asked.

"At first, yes."

The lieutenant inhaled deeply, held the breath, and slowly exhaled.

"I want to thank you for everything you've done for me, Colonel, Major. I didn't know that I wanted this, but maybe the technician was right. I feel that this was inside of me all along and has now been liberated. But I'm a Colonel Walton-trained warrior. I have you to thank for my self-discipline. I will not let the beast take over. I am in command."

Kurtz removed his arm and sat back up. He purposefully looked at Terry and Char, his eyes glistening. "I am in control," he stated confidently.

"As a Pricolici, you'll be able to talk while in Were form. This will help in your training," Char explained. She had heard that they could talk but had fortunately never met one, not in the wild where the Pricolici would have been difficult to handle.

On a *good* day.

"When can we start?" Kurtz pressed.

"We already have." Char watched him closely. She looked for any telltale signs that he was a Were.

Nothing besides the yellow eyes. "By being able to keep yourself from changing, you've passed the first and biggest test. We'll set up some kind of obstacle course in the landing bay and then we'll run you through your paces. I expect you'll bounce off the ceiling a few times before you figure out what you're capable of," Char explained.

"Come on. We've got a lot of shit to do, not the least of which is getting everyone else an implant without turning them into Werewolves." Terry waved at the door to open it and stepped into the hallway.

Dokken was sitting there. "Good call, buddy," Terry told his new pal.

I'm disappointed, TH, the dog started. *We had my arch enemy in hand and you let those creatures protect him. After he drew the blood of your litter? You should be ashamed.*

"Don't be an ass. I already have one of those," Terry replied. "Next time, big man. Next time we'll put that little orange cretin in his place. What do you think of that, boy?"

Dokken barked as he looked up at Terry Henry Walton. The dog's eyes sparkled under the artificial lights.

The door to the quarters closed after Char and Kurtz left the room. "You used to look at me like that," Char said playfully.

"Whoa, buddy! Look at that. Without even trying, you got me in trouble." Terry scratched behind Dokken's ears before turning back to his wife, wrapping an arm around Char's waist.

"You were in trouble well before that dog showed up."

I'm right here, Dokken said.

Char leaned toward the dog. Dokken looked away, falling in behind Char. He trotted alongside Kurtz, warily watching the man.

What are you in for? the dog asked.

"In where?" Kurtz replied as he looked around, wondering where the voice came from. It was the first time anyone had talked with him through the new chip in his head.

Does no one watch movies anymore?

"No, whoever you are. I have never watched a movie." Kurtz looked around him, trying to zero in on the disembodied voice that seemed to project directly into his brain.

This is the hand I've been dealt, Dokken lamented.

CHAPTER TEN

Kim, Kae, Cory, Marcie, Auburn, and Ramses stood in a small group outside the room with the Pod Doc. Ted had brought up the holo screens, put on a headset, and was fully immersed in an intellectual orgy. A normal person would have run screaming from the experience.

Ted looked to be in heaven.

"Smedley says that they're ready any time for the next batch," Kaeden said.

"Dad said to wait. That's what I heard anyway," Kimber replied. Ramses shrugged. The least vocal of the FDG's senior officers, when he did speak, the others listened. Auburn distanced himself from the operational issues within the FDG, except when it came to getting ready for the next op.

He had to rethink his position as the ship and the EI seemed to already supply everything.

But he knew the warriors. If they weren't held account-able, they'd lose everything while operating in the field.

Everything except their weapons. Terry and Marcie had beat it into them that the first and last thing they always checked were their weapons.

The Force's weaponry was antiquated by Federation standards, but it was what they had. Auburn's mind drifted away, thinking of upgrades, improvements, a better, more lethal way ahead.

And he became afraid. There were plenty of ways to die on the ground, but the opportunity to die in space in combat with aliens were magnified a hundredfold. His wife would be in the middle of it all.

"We need to get ship suits for everyone," he blurted, interrupting their conversation. Kim, Kae, and Marcie looked at him oddly.

"In time," Marcie said. They'd been on the ship less than a day.

"No," Auburn replied. "We are in space right now. If anything happens to the ship, we need to be ready. Ship suits will give us time to find safety. I hear that space will kill you as quickly as being trapped underwater. I don't want you to die!"

Kimber smiled at her husband. "Trust me when I tell you that I don't want to die either."

"Check in with Smedley and see what needs to be done and who you need to talk to. Make it happen, Auburn. And that's a good point. Kae, look into weaponry. Kim and Ramses, look at the education schedule and see what the hell we need to learn. We don't know anything about what's out there. We liked to think that we were big and bad, but I expect when we get out there, we're going to find that we're the weak sisters. We'll have to surprise them or this journey will be over before it starts."

"You mean that I have to test fire and evaluate what we might be getting as new weapons? Wow. Sucks to be me." Kae grinned and his eyes darted back and forth as he tried to contemplate what kind of weapons people with space technology might have.

His sister had to rain on his parade.

"Technology that can take us to space, and the only thing you can think of is high-tech weapons." Cory put her hands on her hips and shook her head at the others. "Maybe we can talk with them first."

Kae continued to grin and shrugged unapologetically.

Marcie pursed her lips. "We'll do what we've always done, what we had to do, but this time, we'll have more information and more support. It won't be just us with our asses hanging out."

"I agree with Marcie," Terry Henry Walton said as he strolled up with Char and Kurtz in tow. Cory immediately dropped to a knee to welcome Dokken.

I like her, the dog projected to all of them.

"Of course you do," Terry agreed. "We all do because she keeps us grounded."

Cory ignored the platitudes and continued to scratch Dokken's neck.

"What's the plan, Colonel?" Marcie asked officially.

"Get the Pod Doc cranked up and get back to work bringing our people into the technological fold. If we can communicate better, then I'm all for it. The chips help us to understand the aliens. They'll also help us to communicate in the field. Imagine what our ops would look like if everyone had access to everyone else? No more carrying comm devices. Smedley assures me that we won't have any more inadvertent Pricolici conversions because he knows what to look for."

"What if we find more people who have the Were genes?" Ramses asked.

Terry and Char looked at each other. They'd been thinking that to fight a determined enemy in unknown conditions, they needed Were strength. Char nodded almost imperceptibly.

"We'll ask for volunteers," Terry said softly.

Marcie bit her lip and closed her eyes. "Okay," she replied, before heading back into the space where Ted was fully embroiled with holo screens, scrolling data, and flashing images.

"For fuck's sake, Ted! You're going to give me a seizure!" Marcie yelled, shielding her eyes to pound on his shoulder until he put the holo screens down.

Ted looked angry but continued to scan the data. He muttered something, but Marcie expected he was commiserating with the EI and not talking to her.

"Start running the people through, Ted. No Were conversions, but document who can be converted so we can talk with them, see if we get any volunteers to expand the pack. I'll start sending people to you."

"Already on their way!" Kimber shouted from the corridor.

"Uncle Ted, you will be able to do the mods, right?" Marcie asked, spinning Ted around in his chair. He waved her off.

"Child's play. There is so much more that we can do. I

see the possibilities. I just need to tweak a line of code here or there…" Ted started mumbling to himself as he raised his holo screens.

Marcie pounded on his shoulder again. He lowered the screens and let out a long, exasperated sigh.

"Only the chip and the standard mod everyone else got," Marcie declared as she leaned close to the Werewolf.

"Standard mod? Do you even know what you're saying?" Ted asked in surprise. Marcie stood back, confused.

"There hasn't been two alike! There is nothing standard about this. Now go away and let the adults get to work." Ted waved dismissively as he spun his chair around.

At one hundred and fifty years old, Marcie should have been amused by Ted insulting her youthfulness. She looked mid to late twenties, a blonde-haired and blue-eyed beauty. Lean and hard with a mind shaped toward military operations, and gifts, like being able to see into the Etheric dimension and draw power from it, that helped her lead the Force de Guerre against those who sought to destroy humanity.

And sometimes, *different* targets presented themselves.

Marcie balled her fist and reared back, aiming a haymaker at the back of Ted's head. Terry lunged forward and caught her hand, but he was off-balance.

As she started to swing, the momentum threw TH forward, landing him on top of Ted before rolling to the floor.

"You deal with him!" Marcie snarled before storming from the room.

Ted straightened up and looked oddly at Terry Henry

lying on the floor. "What are you doing down there?" he asked.

Terry sat up and looked coldly at Ted. "The comm chip and basic healing as a first step. Collect your data for recommendations on what other mods can be done, but don't make them. Do you understand me? Don't make me send Felicity in here to watch over you."

Ted scrunched his face as he tried to think of a retort, but nothing came to mind. He waved TH away as he'd done with Marcie. "Fine," he conceded.

Char helped Terry Henry to his feet. "Ted," she said quietly. "Don't make me beat the living crap out of you." She let that sink in before continuing. "*Again.*"

Ted put his head down and watched his screens. His eyes flicked to Char and back to the monitors as he waited for her to go away.

"Send the next lot in," Terry said, brushing himself off.

First to step through the door was Valerie and next was Robin. Ted saw the two Vampires and sneered at Terry and Char. "You want me to do the standard mod on the Vampires. Let me see, where will I find one in the system? Oh, that's right, there isn't one!" Ted harrumphed.

Terry and Char held each other back, before deciding it was time to go. They'd had enough of Ted. When there was less technology in his life, he was much easier to get along with. Ted had never understood people, but with the ability to completely immerse himself in technology out of the wildest science fiction, they figured that they'd already lost him.

They figured that Felicity already knew that Ted was gone.

Smedley, my man. Don't give me any new Pricolici, no matter what Ted tells you to do, but keep a list of what mods each person would be best suited for or most easily capable of getting.

>>I accept my orders according to the chain of command on the *War Axe*. Captain San Marino's orders are the first priority followed by those of Colonel Terry Henry Walton and then Colonel Marcie Walton.<<

Thanks, General. Is Dokken on that list anywhere? Terry asked out of the blue.

>>Of course not.<<

All praise to the EI programmers, Terry relayed through his comm chip while smiling.

>>I don't understand,<< Smedley replied.

No need. Thank you for the insights, Smedley. We're going to talk about a lot of stuff later, the future of the FDG kind of stuff. We'll need your input. I hope you can sit in.

>>Although I cannot physically sit in, I can attend and would be happy to.<<

What makes you happy, makes me happy.

>>I'm not exactly sure about that,<< the EI supposed.

Terry closed the link. Valerie was staring at him. "Well?" she asked.

"Take off your clothes and get in the Pod Doc."

"You would like me to undress, and you ask with that tone of voice?" She clicked her tongue and shook her head. "Manners sure aren't the same in space."

"Use the privacy curtain," he told her and pointed, not even smiling at her joke. They walked out. "When you're done, you're done for the day. Tomorrow, we'll spin things up starting in the rec room at oh-seven-hundred."

Terry, Char, and the others left the Vampires, Sergeant Garcia, and three other FDG warriors standing there wondering what was going to happen next.

A few steps down the corridor, TH stopped and turned. "Garcia, monitor the groups as they come through and in-brief them to reduce the anxiety. Make everyone feel comfortable with the process."

Garcia nodded and said, "Yes, sir," even though he had no idea how to do that, having not gone through the process himself.

Valerie didn't feel any different with the comm chip in her, but had to wonder at it. Anything in her body just felt weird, even if it could supposedly translate so that she could understand aliens…and dogs. That was the weirdest part. Growing up, dogs had been rare enough to feel almost magical. Now she could talk with a dog, from what they told her? The idea sent a shiver down her spine. It was kind of creepy, even.

At her side, Robin was moving her arms about in wind-mills, breathing deep, and then started jumping.

"The hell are you doing?" Valerie asked.

Robin laughed. "These upgrades, I mean…damn. Is this how you always feel?"

"Ah, that. Basically, ever since I got Michael's blood, yes. It's like a new body, right?"

"A new body, a new soul. I feel like I could conquer the world."

"Let's stick to conquering whatever planet or spaceship or whatever these guys sic us on."

Robin laughed. "Deal. You think that's how it'll work? They point us at a target, we take it out? Sounds like we're basically a fancy form of heat-seeking missiles."

"I've been wondering. I mean, we came up here for a reason. I'm just not sure yet if that reason is the same reason they wanted us."

"But we'll do our duty?" Robin asked.

"We're here, right? And whatever it is, I trust Michael and BA. Even if we're glorified assassins, I have to imagine that'll mean we're contributing to a stronger Etheric Federation, and therefore, a safer Earth."

"That's all I want," Robin replied.

Valerie turned to her and put a hand on hers. "They'll be fine."

Robin nodded, biting her lip. Leaving her parents in New York couldn't have been easy, but Valerie completely understood her feelings. As much as they loved their friends and family back on Earth, they were meant for big things. They had the power to make a difference in this war, and could never sleep if they just waited on Earth to see what happened.

"You know I'll follow you to the ends of the universe," Robin stated, then clenched her jaw, her eyes looking fierce. "I'll do whatever it takes to keep them safe. Whatever. It. Takes."

With that, Robin turned and stared out at space, losing herself in thought.

Valerie considered her friend, feeling like all of this made sense. All of it, except for one part. She used the comms in her quarters to make a personal call to the one she trusted for advice and guidance.

A familiar face appeared on the screen.

"Michael, you told me there'd be a place for me in space, but I'm not following how this involves me serving under TH." She cleared her throat, not entirely comfortable with this topic. "Don't get me wrong, he's a great leader. But since when did I agree to him being *my* leader?"

Michael frowned as if this should be clear. "He's going to be heading up the Bad Company. You want to serve in the Bad Company, right?"

"Do we?" She shared a confused look with Robin. "We want to kick ass and do our part. Pardon the language."

Michael laughed at that, breaking her sternness for a moment before regaining her composure. "Sorry, it's just… among us, language is something you never have to apologize for. Especially not when the word is ass. You can do better than that."

Valerie raised an eyebrow.

"Right. The Bad Company. They'll be in the shadows. Collecting intel, doing the dirty jobs, the ones that require people of, er, your particular experience. It seemed a natural fit."

Valerie nodded. "I'm not arguing that."

"Are you arguing anything at all, other than your confusion as to why someone should be giving you commands?"

That hurt. Mostly because, as Valerie stood there looking at Michael, she realized it was true. Back home, she had always been the leader, or at least had been ever since breaking out from under her brother and the Duke. Maybe there was something to that thought—she was having issues with any situation that remotely resembled the one she had fought so hard to escape.

But this was her own issue. Her own problem to deal with.

"Thank you, Michael." She turned to go, then paused. "May I be excused?"

Michael smiled. "You'll get the hang of all this eventually. Dismissed, though you don't actually have to ask that."

Valerie nodded, walking off with Robin close on her heels.

"Just like that?" Robin asked.

"They're right," Valerie replied. "TH is smart as hell. His people love him. They follow his orders and get shit done. There's no reason we can't do so too."

"Except that we don't need them. We—"

"No, Robin." Valerie stopped, then glanced around to be sure nobody was nearby. "That's the way I've been thinking too, I'm realizing. But it's wrong. We're part of a larger body now. We might be sharp fingernails or solid fists, but we need the arms and brain and all that to help us strike where it does the most damage."

Robin frowned, but after a moment, nodded. "Fine, but know this…I'm following you, because it's you I know. You I trust. If I follow them, it's only because you say so."

Valerie nodded. "I think that's good enough, for now. But if I die?"

"Fuck you. Don't ever say that."

"Fine. I won't. But you agree this is the right move? Join me in trying not to question it all, please, because if you keep asking questions, so will I. They don't need doubters, they need warriors."

"Then let's warrior the shit out of them."

Valerie frowned, but couldn't keep the smile from forming. "You're weird, but that's why you're awesome."

"Right back at you," Robin replied, spinning on her heels to lead the way down the hallway.

CHAPTER ELEVEN

The FDG's senior leadership had their missions, from logistics, to weapons, to training, which left Terry and Char free to explore the ship.

"How do you know what time it is?" Terry asked.

Char stopped, cocked her head, and then shrugged. Her eyes unfocused as she talked with the EI through the comm chip.

Her face dropped. "How long do you think we've been on board?" she asked.

"A day? Eighteen to twenty hours? I think I should be more tired." Terry raised his eyebrows in expectation of the answer.

"Seven hours," Char said flatly.

"Holy shit." Terry's eyes glazed over. "It's like we're in a time warp. We've had a few fights, conversions, a great steak, and we have an arch enemy! It's been a full day. I wonder what the next seven hours will hold. Where's Dokken?" Terry looked around.

"He's not far. I smell dog." Char sniffed at the air.

The door to the bridge opened and a crewman worked his way past the ship's first couple. They smiled and nodded as he passed.

Terry noted the thick bulkheads and double-door system leading to the bridge. A ship built for war, but outfitted for comfort. As Terry remembered from his Marine Corps days, there was a great deal less action than people thought. When combat came, it was fast and furious. The other ninety-nine percent of the time, it was training and abject boredom.

Terry wanted to learn what war in space was all about. He had no idea, yet he'd been chosen out of all the beings in the universe to lead the direct-action arm of the Bad Company.

Char was blocking the door with her body as she waited on TH. They'd been married long enough that she knew to let him go when he was lost in thought. She expected it would happen more often with the exponential increase of unknowns in his life.

Terry liked what he liked, and ignorance wasn't one of them.

He blinked back to the present and started forward, rubbing his body across Char's as if trying to squeeze through a too-small space.

Three people could have walked through the door side by side without touching each other. Char chuckled at her husband's mischievous smile.

They found the captain watching them. Terry tried to look embarrassed, but he wasn't. Being back on a warship made him feel like a young Marine again. The surge of energy as they sailed from the safety of their home port into harm's way, ready to disembark under fire.

Then kick ass and take names. So invigorating.

Terry waited until Char was at his side before approaching Captain San Marino.

Micky's position was on a pedestal overlooking the consoles where various crew interacted with screens both two and three-dimensionally. Terry and Char looked up at the captain.

"Master of your domain?" Terry asked.

"Jack of all trades, master of none," Micky replied. "There's a lot that goes on to fly this bad boy around space. You might think that space is a really big place, and the chance of hitting something is small. If that were only the case. Let me show you how we manhandle the *War Axe* through space."

Terry and Char listened intently as the captain walked through the systems and an hour later, Terry understood quite clearly how much he didn't know. By the end, the captain could see it on their faces.

"Breathing the jet stream isn't easy," Micky said sympathetically.

"Were you ever this stupid when it came to space flight?" Terry asked. Char jabbed him in the ribs. The captain hesitated. "Lie to me, then."

"I was raised with this stuff, born to it, I guess you could say. Smedley will help you process it and fill in the blanks when something doesn't make sense. Spend the time with him that you need, both of you. I think you'll find that we follow the laws of physics, but our understanding is a little more in depth than what you were taught."

"I'll say. Thanks, Skipper," Terry said earnestly, holding out his hand. The two men shook and then the captain shook Char's hand.

"Skipper?"

"A Marine term, captain of the boat or a Marine captain. I call all captains Skipper. I hope you don't mind."

"Not at all, Terry. You are an interesting character and I'm sure we are going to…what's the term? Kick down some doors together."

"I would like to think so, and I'd much rather do that than have someone kicking down our doors."

"You might want to rest up. Space is tiring," the captain cautioned.

Terry and Char couldn't argue with the captain. Eight hours and they were ready to pack it in for the night.

"Tonight's meeting is canceled. Thank God. Is anyone else still up?" Marcie sat with her elbows on her knees and her head in her hands.

"Joseph and Petricia. I saw them heading toward the hangar deck," Kae said. "They're like little kids playing with new toys."

"Wouldn't you?" Kae asked, taking a seat next to his wife, stretching languidly before rubbing her back.

"I feel like a kid who's lost her toys." Marcie sighed, closed her eyes, and leaned into Kae's strong fingers.

"It hasn't come back yet?"

"Not a single doorway opening into the fog that is the Etheric. I'm starting to worry. It's like being blind."

"I can't imagine," Kae sympathized. And he couldn't because he'd never touched the Etheric in a way that he could sense. His nanocytes pulled power from the other dimension, but they did that of their own accord.

It was the genius of the Kurtherians and their technology.

Marcie abruptly stood. "Come on. Let's see what Uncle Ted can do. This is his kind of challenge." She held out her hand and Kae took it.

He had no intention of being left behind.

"Did you ever imagine anything like this?" Joseph said as he used one finger to push the hair over Petricia's ear. She smiled back. They had discovered the ship's store and were wearing jeans and button-down shirts.

It was the first time in forever that either had dressed in something other than black leather.

The sun had caused them intense pain. Only leather had protected them. But they didn't need it any longer. Nor was there any sun to bother them.

Petricia leaned close to a porthole beside the vast doors that opened from the hangar bay to space. There were energy fields to keep the atmosphere in, as well.

When something could kill as quickly as space, redundancy was built in.

The Vampire looked at the star field beyond. She planted her face against the clear material. Glass but not glass. Petricia cupped her hands around her eyes to block out the light behind her.

"It's incredible," she whispered.

Joseph squeezed in next to her and together they looked at the stars. Petricia finally turned away, leaning against the forward bulkhead and sighing. She lifted one foot and put it against the wall. She appeared much younger than her century in age.

"Space suits you," Joseph said.

She nodded, but wasn't looking for pleasantries. "Terry Henry saved our lives, in more ways than one."

"I'm from the old country and adhere to the tradition, in my own way, but I owe TH a blood debt that I'll never be able to repay. I will follow him to the end of the universe and back. The best part is that he never takes it for granted." Joseph took Petricia's hands and pulled her to him. "What a life we have."

"I don't want any other." Petricia smiled and put her hand on Joseph's cheek. "I'm curious what's next for us, although you're right. It doesn't matter. We'll do what we need to do. For honor. For Terry Henry and Char."

The two Vampires kissed gently before strolling across the open landing area of the great hangar within the *War Axe*. They had nowhere to be and all the time in the galaxy to get there.

Valerie and Robin stood at the entrance to engineering, mystified at this marvel of a ship. It was unlike anything they had ever come close to seeing back on Earth.

"No regrets?" Valerie asked with a glance at Robin. She knew the younger woman had left behind a lot to come on this journey.

Robin simply shook her head, then gave a wave to one of the engineers who had noticed them and nodded their way.

"I mean…you feel like you came for the right reasons and all?"

This time, Robin frowned, confused, before turning to Valerie. "Holy shit…you think I came because of you."

Valerie blinked, caught off-guard. "Um, you kinda did. I mean, you wouldn't be here if not for me."

"That's two very different things, Val." Robin leaned against the wall, folding her arms across her chest. "I didn't leave my parents behind to come gallivanting after an old flame. Damn, is that what you think of me? I'm here just like you. I know I have something special, and I'm willing to devote my power and skills to making Earth a safer place. If safest place means fighting from the stars, so be it."

Valerie took a moment to process this, then nodded. "So you're just…like…a mini version of me."

Robin laughed and hit her in the arm. "Screw you. You're an older version of me. How about that?"

"I'll take it. Consider me honored."

"It's annoying though, isn't it?" Robin asked.

"What is?"

"This whole having to prove ourselves all over again. It's like we just finished saving everyone's damn lives, putting our part of the world together again, and then we leave, starting over."

"You heard the general back there. Everyone starts over."

Robin nodded thoughtfully. "Ever feel like you're always starting over, though?"

"All the time."

"And what about those other FDG folks?" Robin scoffed. "Micky… Our Micky was twice that man's size and five times as intimidating."

"The leather jacket with a devil patch certainly helped in that regard," Valerie agreed, nodding. Thoughts of him led to others back home, bringing a longing to speak with Sandra to her heart. She pushed it aside, realizing those types of feelings were likely to come more than she would like, and it was best to learn to ignore them early on. Instead, she tried to focus on the here and now. "All those FDG folks get together in the ring, who do you think would win?"

"You mean, excluding TH of course?"

Valerie considered this, then nodded. "They all look up to him so much, they'd be too scared about hitting him and pissing him off to land a shot."

"I'd say give them more credit than that, but…I see the way they look at me…like I'm a child!"

"You tell me the next person to say something, to treat you like a child even, and I'll knock them on their ass."

Robin smiled. "It…it's been mostly in the eyes."

"Well, if it happens. You've done more for Earth than most people I know. Considering the fact that I seem to know *a lot* of heroes nowadays, that's saying something." For a moment, Valerie paused, then assessed her friend. "What we talked about before though, we're cool?"

"You forget, I was the one who insisted we just be friends, that—"

"God, not that!" Valerie cringed, not wanting to ever bring up that subject again. "I mean, about give and take. About fitting in with the team."

Robin chuckled to herself, then nodded. "We're on the *War Axe*, after all. Least I can do is remember that and follow orders. Plus, I've been watching TH and that Char lady…I get it."

"You see what the others see?"

Robin nodded, then stood and stretched. "Speaking of starting over, I feel like my body has evolved, you know what I mean?"

"I…" Valerie frowned, looking away.

"Almost got you there. But look at you, not even a sideways glance."

Valerie smiled, her eyes briefly moving across Robin's body, and then she cringed. "Hey, I tried. You can't tell someone not to think about a peach pie and then expect them not to imagine the tempting scent of that pie."

"I'm peach pie?"

Valerie shrugged. "Just an example. Shut up. I'm going to get some training in or sleep, one of the two. You coming?"

Robin laughed and nodded, following her.

"I'd put my money on Garcia, of course," Valerie commented as they walked out of there.

"What?"

"Out of all the FDG. You know, your question about if they all fought. He's our boy, so of course I'd bet on him."

Robin scoffed. "Typical Val, always putting loyalty above practicality."

"Let me guess, you'd go for one of the messed up Weres?"

"No, Val. I'd put my money on you. Don't forget, you and I are FDG now too, right?"

"Tricky," Valerie replied with a laugh, but as they walked, the thought started to sink in. Their old lives really were behind them. A new beginning with the FDG and the Bad Company lay ahead. Damn, she was excited for that.

The Werewolves stood in the corridor outside the Pod Doc space. Felicity was with them. Sue, Timmons, Shonna, and Merrit watched through the open door.

"I think he's going to orgasm," Merrit said.

"You curb that tongue of yours," Felicity drawled without taking her eyes from her husband. After Billy Spires died of old age, his heart giving out in the middle of a Forsaken attack on their home, Felicity was determined to find a husband who she wouldn't outlive. There had been only one choice.

Ted.

She'd sacrificed a lot for him. Her reward was that she wouldn't outlive him.

Unless he made someone angry enough to kill him, which he'd demonstrated that day that he was fully capable of doing.

Felicity couldn't disagree with Merrit's original state-ment. Ted looked obscenely happy. He was a good-looking man, a shade over six feet tall, brown hair and yellow eyes. He always looked to be in shape, but he didn't work out. His Werewolf nanocytes kept him fit.

His Asperger's set him apart.

And she loved him for that. The others tolerated him, and they begrudgingly admitted that Ted was the genius of the group, even though they were all intelligent. No one approached Ted's level.

Not even Terry Henry Walton with his eidetic memory.

"Are we going to just stand here?" Felicity asked. The others shrugged. They had nowhere to be.

Marcie appeared with Kae by her side. She didn't acknowledge the others as she passed.

"Aunts, Uncles," Kaeden told them before adding, "Mother-in-law," for Felicity.

"Uncle Ted," Marcie said as she walked in on the latest group waiting for their chip implants and the basic modifications that the nanocytes would provide. The door opened and a naked warrior stepped out, quickly diving behind the privacy curtain when he saw the colonel standing there.

But she hadn't been looking at him. "Uncle Ted. I can't feel the etheric and I need to. I'm empty without it."

She pounded on his shoulder to get his attention. He dropped the holo screens and she explained again. He held up one finger and went back to his screens.

Marcie snarled and growled, but Kae held her back. "Give him time," he pleaded.

The next warrior climbed into the pod, but the door remained open. The young woman lay there, exposed to the world. She tried to cover up with her hands, but failed. Kae moved the privacy curtain to block the open Pod Doc.

"Get in," Ted told Marcie. She stepped behind the screen, dropped her clothes, and waved at the other woman to get out. She hurried from the pod and Marcie got in. The door closed, and Ted disappeared into his data.

Both groups watched and waited.

CHAPTER TWELVE

Day 2 aboard the *War Axe*

Terry had the FDG standing in formation on the hangar deck. All hands were getting used to their new capabilities. The tac teams stood behind the two platoons with the newest members from the UnknownWorld, Valerie and Robin.

Marcie wore a smile as she looked down at her husband. Kae couldn't ignore it. "Damn that Ted!" he declared.

"Why? Because I'm bigger now? Or because he gave me my sight back?"

"I'm sorry, sweetheart," Kaeden said. "I know it was worth the price, but look at you!"

She stood back and smiled. "Yes. Look at me," she said softly as she struck a pose. She flexed to put her new power on display.

"Magnificent," Kae said, smiling to himself, still sore from Marcie's display of her new strength in the privacy of their quarters the previous evening.

"Holy shit, Marcie," Kim said, shaking her head and chuckling quietly. "It's hard to get used to, after all these years."

Marcie winked. She was reveling in the change. She'd been the strongest and fastest of them all. That was before.

She couldn't wait to spar with Terry Henry Walton. Maybe she wouldn't finish flat on her back, gasping for air, as she had nearly every other time. She ended up face-first the rest of the time.

Terry and Char made their entrance with Dokken trotting alongside. Terry rested his hand lightly on the dog's head. Lieutenant Kurtz executed an about-face and saluted.

"I'm glad to see you, Kurtz. Well done on getting everyone here from the rec room. Don't you hate it when the word changes?" Terry joked.

"We do as we're told, except when we don't," the lieutenant replied, as was his custom.

"Oorah, Lieutenant. Take your place." Terry returned Kurtz's salute and the man marched smartly around Terry and Char, taking his position at Char's left.

"At ease!" Terry barked. The warriors snapped to parade rest before relaxing, loosening their shoulders and stretching in place.

"What a glorious day! We awaken not to a sunrise, but a sunset. Earth is a speck receding into the distance behind us. Soon, we'll gate from our solar system to Yollin space where we will access a gate that will take us to the Paladin System where we'll find Onyx Station. Once there, we'll be determining our future."

Terry paced back and forth in front of the platoons,

stopping often to nod at one person or another. He was greeted by eager and determined looks.

"Between now and then, we've got an absolute shit-pot of work to do. You'll be happy to work out because that will be your reprieve from the grind. We have to learn about new peoples, new cultures, new technology, including a little something that Major Kaeden will set up for us for tomorrow. A hand-held railgun, a weapon that takes a small projectile and accelerates it to an insane speed. When it hits, the target vaporizes because of the release of kinetic energy! What's kinetic energy? That's all part of your lessons.

"Auburn tells me that everyone will be issued a ship suit, an emergency environmental suit. It'll keep you alive in the vacuum of space until you can get back to a contained environment. Why can't you breathe out there? More classes. More science. More engineering. Learn that stuff, but there are the important things that we're already good at." Terry waited, but he saw the warriors nod.

"We're good at fucking up bad guys. Consider us as meals on space wheels, delivering shit sandwiches to all corners of the 'verse." Terry thrust his arms in the air and issued his war cry. The warriors joined in.

The large space that was the hangar bay filled with the volume of seventy voices, raised in unison.

"Smedley, I have to say that was most enlightening," Ted said as he leaned back in his chair. "What time is it?"

"It is nine in the morning. You have not slept. You have

not eaten. If you do not eat and rest, I will close out your access to all systems."

"Emergency override, authorization Ted the Magnificent…"

Smedley interrupted. "Stop it, Ted. I let you think you installed that little gem to create a backdoor, but it doesn't. I didn't expect you to try to use it so quickly. I'm putting my foot down," Smedley said over the speakers in the panel.

"You don't have feet," Ted replied, confused.

"Logging you out in three, two, one." The screens went blank and Ted glared angrily at the darkness.

"I'll find a way in the backdoor, or my name isn't Ted the Magnificent," Ted declared.

But your name isn't Ted the Magnificent, Smedley countered through the comm chip.

Ted didn't dignify that with a response. Of course his name was Ted the Magnificent. Who said that he couldn't give himself a name?

Without the stimulus from the computer, Ted felt both hungry and tired. As he walked from the Pod Doc space, he found himself trudging along on his way to the mess deck. He realized that no one else was around. Not the crew or the FDG. He wondered where they'd gone, but not enough to call them using the ship's communications.

He rather enjoyed the solitude. He felt like bacon. He wondered if there would be any.

Captain San Marino slept very little. His place was on the bridge and that was where he spent nearly one hundred percent of his waking hours. The nanocytes that coursed through his veins were designed to help keep him sharp over long periods of time. He was wired to go without sleep.

"When will the gate engines be fully charged?" he asked navigation.

"Thirty more minutes, Captain," a man immersed within a holographic systems map stated. Micky chewed on the inside of his lip as he watched the bridge crew work.

The captain was in charge of the whole ship, but he had section leaders to take care of their business. Engines, Structure, Environmental, and Stores. A commander was over each critical ship system. Four competent, experienced leaders.

That left Micky to drive the boat, which was what he loved to do more than anything else. He'd never taken the *War Axe* into a fight.

He wasn't in a hurry. With the FDG on board, he needed to keep training his people to fight the ship. He needed Terry Henry Walton's people to perform damage control. They needed to be part of the solution, not the problem.

"Spin it down, helm," the captain ordered. The man in the three-dimensional bubble stiffened.

"Captain?"

"Take the gate engines offline. We'll form a gate and transit as soon as we've conducted three successful damage control drills in a row. It won't be perfect, but it has to be good enough. How many times has one of ours been jumped as soon as they exited a gate? The answer is too many times."

The captain tapped the small screen built into the arm of his chair. It rested beneath his right hand where the most common emergency system controls were less than a finger-breadth away.

He opened the ship-wide communication. "All hands. Damage control drill will begin in fifteen minutes. Review your procedures and prepare to assume your emergency stations."

The bridge crew silently went about their duties. He watched a few surreptitiously expose the hoods of their ship suits. When the alarm sounded, they'd be suited in no time. He didn't begrudge them that, but he couldn't have anyone taking shortcuts.

"Stow your hoods, people."

Without looking, the crew casually secured their hoods inside the rear neck pouches. Micky was proud of his crew. They were eager and motivated. No captain could ask for more.

He tapped his right finger once and swiped it across the screen. The emergency klaxons pounded an ugly staccato at the outset, followed quickly by a long bass tone. He activated ship-wide comm. "This is a drill. This is a drill. All hands man your stations. Smedley, report the damage and dispatch damage control."

The instant Micky raised his finger from the panel, Smedley's liquid tones filled the air. "Hull breach at frame one-three-four, level five, section six. All hands, hull breach. Secure and recover. This is a drill."

The captain visualized the bustle within the ship as crew members ran down the passages, using the port side to run aft, that was, the left side of the ship as one looked toward the nose. Aft was the rear of the ship. In emergencies, the crew ran forward on the starboard side and ran to the rear using the main port, or left side, corridor. Those simple rules kept the crew from running into each other.

The lateral passageways offered a way for a crew member to get from one side of the ship to the other. Going in the right direction was important to minimize the time it took to get on station or get into a position for damage control.

The ship was filled with repair bots standing by. They conducted most of the repairs within damaged sections. That was the plan anyway. The *War Axe* had never been in battle, had never had a breach.

From a relative standpoint, the ship wasn't that big. The captain could run from the bridge to the engine compartment in less than a minute, but the engines were twelve decks below the bridge. The captain could run to the bow of the ship in four minutes if he worked at it. Six, if he took it easy.

Why he would be running forward, he wasn't sure. He'd done it during drills, but his place was on the bridge. In case of a hull breach, doors would slam shut to minimize the loss of atmosphere, creating self-contained zones throughout the ship. Then it would be each section for themselves until the crew and the repair bots fixed the problems, and the people could link up again.

The ship ran itself. Mostly.

Micky's role was to manage it all. It was best for him to

stay where he was. He casually snapped open the pouch at the back collar of his ship suit and pulled the hood over his head. It settled into place, and thin magnetic strips sealed together with a hook and loop backup. The hood filled with air and became a transparent bubble around the captain's head.

He noted that he was last to complete the emergency action. Fifteen seconds had passed since the klaxons first sounded. The target was five seconds. Next time, he'd set a better example.

He tapped a finger on his arm chair console.

"Secure the bridge," Micky said. The double bulkhead doors slammed into place, isolating the bridge from the rest of the ship. "Systems, report."

A Yollin worked at the systems station. A holo image of the ship floated in front of him. He used his hands and mandibles to manipulate the image. He was from an upper-class family and had four legs. He was the only member of the bridge crew without an environmental suit.

The Yollin didn't use one and the Federation was good with that. If the captain had been given a choice? He'd still wear his. Many in his crew were young and were still invincible, in their minds. Micky San Marino's job was to protect them from themselves.

"Smedley," the captain said quietly. "Schedule a ship suit confidence exercise for later today. We're taking our crew and passengers on a spacewalk."

A capital idea, Captain! Smedley replied directly into Micky's brain.

K'thrall turned his whole body to look at the captain. "Damage control bots are operating at maximum efficiency," he said in his clicks and tones that the translation chip turned into words the humans could understand.

"What about the crew? Did anyone get trapped behind the barriers?"

"Five of our passengers only," K'thrall reported.

"How in the hell did this happen?" Terry beat his fist against the bulkhead that sealed him and Char into the space. His clear bubble helmet fogged as he complained.

Marcie paced as she tried to communicate with Lieutenant Kurtz by using the comm chip to speak through the EI. Kimber and Timmons leaned against the wall, more accepting of the situation, yet uncomfortable with it. Dokken danced back and forth as he tried not to get run over.

"Smedley Butler runs the exercises. If you had the senior leadership of a unit all in one place at one time, you would cut them off, too," Char suggested.

Terry stepped back from the hatch. "It's exactly what I'd do and now that we have chips, my man Smedley knows where we are at all times, don't you, Smedley?"

They all looked around as if the EI would materialize. Silence greeted them.

"We're cut off," Marcie said, throwing her hands up in frustration. Char joined Timmons and Kimber leaning against the wall.

"If I had reviewed the procedures, I'd know what we're supposed to be doing." Terry's memory had never failed him. If he read something, he remembered it forever. He still casually read Shakespeare by reading each page within his mind, flipping them casually to read on.

He stood with his feet shoulder width apart, knees slightly flexed as if getting ready to start calisthenics or engage in hand-to-hand combat. He closed his eyes and started looking through everything he had read about the ship. Terry had reviewed the maps in the rec room as soon as they came on board.

He knew *exactly* where they were. And that didn't help him one bit. The bulkheads of the *War Axe* were designed to isolate the smallest space possible around a breach to leave as much of the intact ship accessible as possible.

It made sense, unless you were trapped in the small space that had been designated for the breach. Finally, Terry joined Char, slammed his back against the wall, and slid to the floor. The others sat down as well. Terry looked back and forth and sighed into his bubble helmet, fogging it momentarily.

When it cleared, they could see he was chuckling.

"The entire senior leadership. One grenade could take us out."

"Kae is out there with them. And Ramses, and Cory, and Joseph, and everyone else. Damn, Dad! Mom always said you were a control freak."

"Don't put this on me! You know he's a control freak."

"He is," Timmons added.

Dokken panted and bobbed his head as if he wanted to say something. Terry tapped his head. "I can't hear you, boy," Terry apologized. He petted the huge German Shepard's head, finishing with a good scratch behind the dog's ears. Dokken sighed, worked his way between Terry and

Char, and laid down, with half his body in each of their laps.

"How much room do you think there is? I would have never taken you for a lapdog," Terry said as he and Char absentmindedly stroked Dokken's thick hair. He made for a warm armrest.

"So now we wait," Terry lamented.

"Kaeden and the others will do just fine. The FDG is well trained, thanks to that Colonel Walton guy," Kimber offered with a smile. Char bit her lip to keep from laughing. She was ready to get out of the cramped space, but would never share that with her husband.

"I'm not good at waiting," Terry said softly.

CHAPTER THIRTEEN

Valerie and Robin watched the others hurrying around the rec room, taking head counts, checking ship suits, and accomplishing very little besides being active.

"Put on your hoods!" Kae ordered, looking at the two Vampires.

Valerie glared back, but Robin elbowed her in the ribs. "We're supposed to play nice, remember?"

Robin pulled her hood over her face and let it snap in place. The air flow started and positive pressure expanded the bubble around her head. "Funky," she admitted, bobbing to an unheard beat.

Valerie followed suit, clicking the clear plastic material into place. It inflated around her head as air filled the space. She breathed deeply.

"I see what you mean," she replied. The air was clean and the pressure almost forced the air into her lungs. She wondered if one was unable to breathe if the suit would keep them alive. She determined to ask, just in case she needed to kill an enemy who was wearing something comparable.

The Vampire flexed and stretched. The ship suit already felt like a second skin. "I thought space suits would be more bulky," Valerie admitted. "What do you think it'll be like fighting in space?"

Robin shrugged. "I'll probably still kick your ass."

"Hardly," Valerie replied. "Need I remind you that I took out the entire clan of wannabe ninjas that turned you into what you are."

"With my help, and I resent that." Robin turned to put her hands on the wall, stretching. "They taught me some sword techniques, but you've taught me more than they ever could."

"Thanks."

The captain tapped his panel. "This concludes the drill. Department heads and Force de Guerre senior leadership please report to the captain's conference room for a debrief."

Micky unsnapped his helmet and took a deep breath. He always did it the same way, as if the air on the bridge was better than the clean air of the suit. He could already hear the small generator working to recharge the compressed gas cylinder. It was capable of pulling air from a near vacuum, but it took time.

The captain climbed down and walked from one person to the next of his bridge crew to thank them for their efforts. The most important thing to him was that they took it seriously. No one was running through the motions.

He had seen that on his last ship, but he hadn't been the captain. He tried to talk to the captain, but she wouldn't listen, stating that her culture did not give awards when people did their jobs. Morale suffered. The ship had a high efficiency rating, which confirmed in her mind that she was doing the right thing.

Micky wasn't convinced. He liked his way. He slapped the helmsman on the back and gave him the thumbs up. The man pointed to the holo image of the systems, specifically to the gate engine. "Not yet, wild man, but soon."

The bulkheads lifted back into the overhead, and Terry vaulted to his feet. Then stopped to listen to the captain's announcement.

Smedley, can you have Kaeden join us for the debrief?

>>**He is already on his way, sir.**<<

"There you are, you slimy worm! You stay in my head unless I tell you otherwise, you understand?" Terry snarled aloud.

>>**Ooh, Colonel, um, how about no, and say we did?**<<

I'm now hating your programmer, you sandy little butt-hole! You smegma-infested, warthog-faced buffoon. You decrepit pile of Klingons circling Uranus! Terry stated boldly in his best mindspeak.

>>**Lashing out! I get that more often than I care to admit. But I can't change standing Federation orders. I**

hope you understand, although you can lash me with your tongue whip as much as you'd like, if it makes you feel better,<< Smedley said happily.

Terry turned his head sideways and pounded on it as if trying to drive water from the ear on the opposite side.

"I hope you fall out of there so I can stomp on you!" Terry declared.

>>I'm afraid if the comm chip fell out of your ear that way, Colonel, you would be in no condition to stomp anything. The captain is in the conference room, as is Major Kaeden and the four department heads.<<

Terry stopped what he was doing as the others watched him curiously. "We need to find some bad guys quickly because I need to beat the shit out of somebody," Terry declared as he straightened up and marched smartly toward the aft section of the ship where the stairway to the bridge was located.

"Do you think it's settled?" Timmons asked, although he knew the answer. He'd been in the pack long enough to know.

"Not at all," Char said, confirming his suspicion.

When's lunch? I'm hungry. Can we have more beef? I like beef. Much better than bistok. Please? More? Dokken pleaded.

"No," Terry said, cutting the dog off. "We won't be eating for a while, buddy, because we've got some stuff to do first."

An orange flash appeared ahead as Wenceslaus disappeared down a side corridor. Dokken roared the war cry of his people and darted forward, sliding through the intersection and slamming into the opposite bulkhead. He continued to bark, froth flying from his dog face as he raced after his arch enemy.

An orange cat.

Terry stopped at the side corridor to watch Dokken disappear around the corner at the far end.

"I'm not sure he would know what to do with the good king if he caught him," Char said.

"I suspect you're right." Terry looked from one face to the next. Timmons, a Werewolf, far older than Terry Henry. Kimber, Terry and Char's adopted daughter. And Marcie, their daughter-in-law, married to Kimber's brother. "What the fuck are we doing?" Terry asked abruptly.

"What do you mean?" Char asked, suddenly concerned at her husband's change of mood.

"We're going to a distant galaxy where we're going to be a mercenary group, working for pay that we have no idea what it's worth, doing the bidding of a person we've never met."

"Because Bethany Anne asked. That's why. She's been out there. She's seen the bad guys, and to make the universe a better place, she left her people in charge. They know about us from Akio. If he is confident that we're the right ones for the job, then I have no doubt that we are. This isn't about any of that, my lover. This is about control. You don't know, and that scares the crap out of you because you're thinking of all the worst possibilities. Like being trapped in a small compartment while everyone you know is out there, doing the best they can without you."

Terry closed his eyes and dug deeply into himself. He felt like the first time he'd gone into combat as a private first class. He followed orders, until he realized that he was good at it, then he left the others behind as he became a pure combat Marine.

He had no idea what the next battle was going to look like. He no longer carried the burden of a dystopian Earth on his shoulders, but the burden of an unknown universe. It was too much to ask of his great strength.

But even Bethany Anne had help.

The help of those closest to her. And the help of Terry Henry Walton and his well-trained people. He smiled at his purple-eyed, Werewolf wife and gently put his hand against her cheek.

"Let's go see what the captain has to say about the ship's performance."

"You want to know how the Force did," Char said, happy that Terry had worked through his issues with having to control his environment and the things that impacted the people he cared about.

"Of course," he conceded, before turning and continuing toward the bridge. Dokken's barking receded into the distance.

Captain San Marino watched what seemed like an endless stream of people file into his conference room. They filled the seats and lined the walls.

The four department heads joined the captain at the conference table. Kae had taken a seat, but Kurtz refused to sit because there weren't enough seats for everyone.

Valerie sat at the table next to Kae because she knew it annoyed him.

The look on his face told the captain everything he needed to know about the Vampire's relationship with the major.

When Terry, Char, Marcie, Timmons, and Kimber arrived, there were two seats left at the table and standing room only for the rest. Terry looked at the group. The captain and Kae both looked like they needed someone to throw them a lifeline.

"Skipper! Did we win?" Terry asked happily, watching the faces of those in the room. Tensions were high.

The captain looked confused. Terry was back to being Terry. He saw the situation and had come up with a plan of action to defuse tensions. The others didn't know what his plan was, but they saw the confidence he exuded.

He didn't need to beat the shit out of anyone. Terry Henry only needed to solve a problem that only Terry Henry could solve.

"What do you say we take this to the chow hall, get some of Jenelope's fine cooking, and talk about how devious that Smedley Butler is?" Terry worked his way around the table, slapping people on the back as he went. He shook the hands of the department heads.

The environmental head was MacEachthighearna, a broad-shouldered man of Scottish descent. Terry butchered the man's name, so he told Terry to call him Mac.

Engines were run by Suresha, a tall and sickly thin woman. She was nearly as tall as Aaron, who stood against the wall with Yanmei in front of him.

Blagun Lagunov led the structure department. "Did we close the breach before losing anyone?" Terry quipped.

"My bots worked magnificently, but not before the FDG command team was vented to space." Terry hesitated before making a show of pinching his arm.

"We got better," he replied.

Oscar Wirth was in charge of the *War Axe* stores. "I never get to have any fun," he said. "Thanks for bringing the beef. That will be a big hit. We've got the replicators working on the formula and structure now."

Terry leaned close and whispered conspiratorially, "I'm not sure what to say to that, but don't tell Auburn." He pointed to his son-in-law, who was standing with his arms crossed.

"We've already talked. He said that he'll be able to tell the difference, so that is the standard we must meet." The man nodded confidently.

"I look forward to your victory in the taste test," Terry told him. The captain stood and breathed a sigh of relief as he took Terry's hand. He moved close. "Thanks for that."

"Any time. Thank you for not flying us into an asteroid and ending our existence," Terry replied good-naturedly.

"It's hard to argue with that."

"To the chow hall!" Terry bellowed.

"To the mess deck!" the captain translated for his people.

Terry waited until everyone had gone in because he always ate last. Kae pulled him aside.

"Fucking Robin…" Kae started, but Terry stopped him.

"Michael explained it to me," Terry started. "Imagine if you had vampiric speed in addition to everything else the nanocytes provide, but you were left in the Wasteland by yourself. How much would you trust other people?"

Kae's brow furled as he thought about what his father had said. Terry and Char had found him on the edge of the Wasteland, having survived an attack by raiders. What if he had the strength of a Vampire? Things would have been different.

Far different.

"I think I understand."

"Yeah. Cut them some slack. We all have a long ways to go and I think when we get there, we're going to want her and Valerie to be on our side, just like we'll want to be on their side. With great power comes great responsibility, but what if you've only been responsible for yourself? Come on, Kae, let's get some chow."

Joseph and Petricia had been in the captain's conference room, along with the rest of Char's pack, including Felicity. Ted hadn't made it because he locked himself in the Pod Doc space to conduct research, according to him.

"What do you think that was all about?" Petricia asked as she chewed her goulash, slowly, savoring each bite. "Is it just me or does the food taste better?"

"I think since we are freed from the blood bond, our eyes are opened to a world of new sensations. As for the conference room, classic Terry Henry. I love it!"

Petricia blinked slowly as she continued to chew. Joseph watched her with great interest. Huge blocks of time were missing from his life. The years that he slept. The decade that he and Petricia had been captured and kept under anesthesia as part of the blood trade. They had survived, but to Joseph, he'd spent scant years with his wife, although long decades had passed since they married.

"We need a honeymoon," he said.

"What better than a trip to the stars?" she offered.

"I think we're going to find that when we get there, we're going to be running. Always running. That's Terry's cure for everything. Feeling good? How about forty miles? Feeling bad? Make it fifty. Let's climb the outside of a building! That will be fun." Joseph laughed as he watched Kae walk in ahead of Terry.

Both men looked comfortable, where Kae had looked angry when he pulled Terry aside.

"I wonder what that was about," Joseph said before shrugging. "All's well that ends well, I guess."

Petricia turned serious. "When do you think training will start?"

"In earnest?" Joseph answered the question with a question. "I'm surprised that it hasn't started already. So let me say, soon. Very soon, and it'll be hard. I expect no less from Terry and Char."

The captain was waiting for Terry. "I insist," he said, motioning Terry ahead of him in line.

"No sweat," Terry said, much to everyone's surprise.

"You're the ranking officer. I'm on your boat and it's good to see one of you fleet boys stepping up."

"How many so-called fleet boys do you know?" the captain asked.

"Counting you? That would be one."

Char raised one eyebrow. "You're in rare form today, TH. Maybe we should lock you behind a bulkhead more often," she teased.

"Or maybe someone with sparkling purple eyes showed me the light?" Terry pulled Char close to him.

A wooden spoon smacked him on the arm. "What the...?"

"You're holding up the line," Jenelope said from beneath a dark scowl. Terry looked back. Only the captain was behind him and he shook his head and raised his hands. "None of that funny business in here. Get your food, eat, and get out."

"Yes, ma'am," Terry replied, straightening up as he and Char hurried through, loading their trays to near-over-flowing. The captain followed loading a far smaller portion on his tray.

When they sat down, the captain started talking while Terry and Char seemed to be engaged in a speed-eating contest.

"This afternoon, we're having all hands practice space-walking using only their ship suits."

Terry stopped mid-bite. "I love that idea." He looked around, found Kae, and waved him over. "Can you set up the weapons demo for this afternoon?"

"Yes, I can," he said happily. He hurried away. "Marcie!"

"How did we do, Skipper?" Terry asked, turning serious.

"Just fine. The landing force's role is simple. Stay out of the way of the crew. Your group did that, although they were slow getting their hoods up," the captain said, cocking his head to emphasize his point. "The next phase will be for all your people to get into the shuttle pods. Just in case we lose the ship, we don't have to lose everyone aboard."

"We can do that. I'll have them running around the ship right after chow. They need to learn their way and we need to run."

Joseph tipped his chin to Petricia. "Told you," he said.

Cory and Ramses joined the two Vampires. The four department heads slid further down the table to make room for the woman who looked like Char's younger sister but with glowing blue eyes. She thanked them with a smile. "What are you up to?" she asked.

"We are engaged in the non-contact sport of people-watching," Joseph replied.

Cory pursed her lips as she looked around at the group. "Are you seeing anything good?"

"The people are happy. So much we don't know about our future and they're happy," Joseph said as if he didn't believe what he was seeing.

"We have nice beds, good food, and we're all in it together. My dad is all about bonding through shared misery. Give us a good crisis any day and I'll show you how tight a team can get," Cory said, mimicking Terry's voice.

"Be careful what you ask for," Joseph intoned.

CHAPTER FOURTEEN

The entirety of the FDG stood in formation on the hangar deck. The bridge crew was on the hangar deck with them, except for the Yollin, K'thrall.

Werewolves, Weretigers, and Vampires, although Joseph and Petricia stayed as far away from Valerie and Robin as they could. Cory and Ramses assumed the role of peacekeeper and stayed next to the new additions to the team.

Two platoons with Kurtz out in front. Terry stood before him at attention as everyone waited on Captain San Marino, who was watching from the shadows until Terry gave him the thumbs up. After an appropriately respectful amount of time, Terry signaled.

Micky stepped off smartly and headed straight for the center of the hangar bay. When he was five feet from Terry, he nodded.

"HOODS!" Terry roared. He reached behind his head and pulled his hood around to the front in a single swift motion. It snapped in place. The captain was close behind as Smedley sounded the emergency klaxons. The great hangar doors started to open. With the emergency force-field deactivated, the air vented to space. Two warriors went down as they didn't have their hoods in place. Those next to them helped, saving the warriors' lives.

An animal's growl rumbled deep in Terry's throat. "You're better than this," he whispered at his people.

The captain appeared by his side. "You ready?" he asked.

"Now is as good a time as ever," Terry replied.

"Smedley, remove the artificial gravity in the hangar bay."

The people remained where they were for a moment, then they started drifting and bouncing off each other. Warriors being warriors, they pushed off to see how fast they could get themselves going.

"Physics may not be their strong suit," Terry suggested. "But they like practical application. I expect they'll understand the basics of Newton's laws pretty soon."

They watched a warrior start flailing as he approached the ceiling at a high rate of speed. To his credit, he was able to spin around and hit feet-first. He smashed into the heavy composite material like a bug hitting a windshield. He recoiled from the impact, only half-conscious.

But he was newly enhanced and his nanocytes were already at work repairing the damage that he'd done to his body.

Char tried swimming, but without any resistance, everyone simply floated, although Terry and the captain remained firmly on the deck. They were wearing special boots with weak magnetic locks. Char had them as well, but she hadn't activated them. Terry released his locks and let himself float free.

Micky soon joined him. For fifteen minutes, the group floated around the inside of the hangar bay. Terry tried moving and realized what a disadvantage it would be to fight in such an environment. Whoever fired first and most accurately would win the day. He added that to the training regimen he was building in his mind—zero-gee marksmanship.

"Smedley," the captain said within his helmet. "Please bring the gravity to ten percent of Earth standard." Immediately, the free-floating mob headed toward the deck, but slowly, deliberately.

The EI incrementally increased the gravity until they were back to normal, everyone had their feet on the ground, but environmental had not been restored. The warriors and crew remained within their ship suits with their hoods inflated around their heads.

Kae signaled he was ready and they moved to the open bay doors, to the edge of space, and stood, looking into the darkness at the infinite stars. Terry gave them all a moment to appreciate it before Kae began the demo.

Handheld railguns, plasma rifles, and the multi-handgun which fired both kinetic projectiles and sonic blasts. It gave the FDG a non-lethal capability.

As the warriors cycled through firing a few shots of each into space, Kaeden approached Terry carrying a box.

"Found this in the armory," he said loudly, trying to be heard. When they pressed their helmets together, Terry could hear him without using their comm chip.

"What is it?" Terry asked. Kae shrugged and handed it over.

There was an envelope taped to the top. Terry opened it and pulled out the card inside.

TH: use this wisely in defense of the Empress' ideals. Trust your moral compass as it has served you well and will continue to serve you and yours. This is called a Jean Dukes Special. It is a warrior's weapon. Michael

The rest of the note contained specifics about the weapon. Five thousand rounds fired at various velocities. How to clean and reload the weapon, the basics that Terry found compelling. The more he read, the more he liked.

He would be able to key it to his bio-signature so a weapon of that magnitude could not be used by others. Terry decided that he'd key it to everyone in his inner circle, so they could use it, should he fall.

Terry opened the box and found a pistol inside, a bulky pistol with a selector lever that went from one to eleven. Terry hefted the firearm. It was heavy, but not prohibitively so. Terry took it to a position on the firing line. He set the lever to three, having no idea why he'd ever want to shoot at the lowest setting.

He pulled the trigger and sent a projectile into space. Then another and another, dialing up by one each time. The kick increased with each new level. He skipped ten and went straight to eleven. TH braced himself and leaned forward. When he pulled the trigger, the pistol tried to leap from his hand. A searing pain shot through his shoulder.

He looked at the weapon in surprise before a grin split his face. "I love this thing! Wherever you are, Michael, thank you." When he turned around, he saw the warriors cheering, but it made no sound that he could hear.

Terry cradled the pistol in both hands as he walked around the formation.

Char and the pack wore smiles because Terry must have looked like a little kid at Christmas. Valerie had her eyes on the weapon. She said something. Terry signaled that he couldn't hear.

She squinted as she concentrated.

"Can I try it?" she asked. He heard her directly in his head. He selfishly wanted to say no, but decided against it. The only ones with the strength to fire the weapon besides himself were Marcie and the Vampires. He didn't think Char could handle it at the highest setting. She was Werewolf strong, but the pistol bordered on the ludicrous.

Terry pointed to Marcie and Joseph. Marcie grinned and hurried to him. Joseph shook his head. He'd never been a fan of weapons. Valerie and Robin came too as Terry returned to the edge of space.

He handed the pistol to Valerie. "Try it on nine first." She dialed it in, took aim, and fired. He watched her expression closely. She adjusted her grip and fired again. Then dialed it to eleven and sent a projectile into space. She winced as Terry had, but with a simple roll of her shoulder, she looked fully recovered.

Terry's shoulder still hurt as the nanocytes worked their magic. Valerie handed the pistol to Robin, who fired two at nine and one at eleven. The Vampires looked pleased.

"We want one, too," Valerie said.

"This was a gift from Michael. I'll try to find out where

he got it and see what we can do to order a few more." She nodded tersely, and the two Vampires walked away.

Marcie dialed it to five, fired, then seven, and fired again. She improved her stance with each. She fired once at nine, and then set it to eleven. She tucked her elbow in tightly, and although she couldn't aim well, she minimized the impact on her shoulder.

Watching the JDS fire at the max setting was a treat. Terry couldn't wait to see it in action. He expected that it could level a building. Not something to be used indiscriminately.

If he had to order a final protective fire? The Jean Dukes Special had no rival.

The captain said something into his helmet, and the forcefield appeared. The process of restoring atmosphere to the hangar bay began. The people moved away from the edge as the massive hangar doors slid soundlessly into place.

Terry slapped Kaeden on the back. "Nice demo and thanks," he told his son. Kaeden looked at his father's new pistol. Terry took note. "The fewer there are of these in the galaxy, the better off we'll be."

"I think you're probably right," Kae replied.

Micky folded his helmet back and took a deep breath, signaling the others that the air was good enough. When the helmets were removed and the air once again transmitted sound, Terry and Micky stood side by side.

"First squad, first platoon, report to the chow hall and bring down the meal that our wonderful chef has prepared. Second platoon, join with the bridge crew and break out the tables and chairs."

Micky cupped his hands around his mouth. He wasn't used to projecting his voice as TH was so adept at doing. "Open locker seven and set up to welcome our guests!"

Terry and the captain showed a united front as they entered the crowd to make sure the two groups intermingled.

Terry found Lieutenant Kurtz, pulling him aside while greeting people. The colonel's face turned sour. "You get those two stupid fuckers who didn't get their helmets on quickly enough and get them to unfuck themselves. What an embarrassment, for fuck's sake. There aren't enough of us out here that we can afford for anyone to die stupid."

The lieutenant had been thinking the same thing. He'd already talked with both during the weapons demonstration, but the colonel's anger further drove the point home.

"Worst to first, sir. Their performance standard is that they'll have their hoods up before anyone else next time. I would ask that any time you see them, make them pull their helmets on. It'll be second nature to them," Kurtz promised.

"It needs to be second nature to every warrior, Lieutenant. Me, you, the pack, the Vampires. All of us."

Kurtz nodded once and hurried in search of the platoon leader and the offending members' squad leaders. It was the FDG's way. Everyone in the chain of command would suffer for the transgressions of the front lines. Terry insisted it was a training issue. If the warriors didn't perform, it had to be because they weren't trained well enough or they'd lost their focus. Both reflected more on the leadership than on the individuals.

In Kurtz's mind, he just got his ass chewed up one side

and down the other. In the immortal words of militaries throughout the ages, shit rolls downhill.

Yol Space

P'tok sat in the captain's chair, anxiously clicking his mandibles. The Yollin manning the renegade ship were silent, afraid to move, careful breathing so they didn't ignite the captain's fire.

His volatility was well-known in their circles, but he delivered. In their loose conglomerate of thieves, he always returned with the most merchandise.

The civilized world called it plunder. Stolen goods. But as long as there was a market for it, there'd always be people like P'tok who would acquire it.

Plus there was always the gold. No matter where P'tok took his ship in the Federation, gold was legal tender. All ships carried it as the universal currency. He considered the gold as gravy. The cargo paid for the ship and its crew.

P'tok scratched around his carapace. Environmental controls had to be off or the chef was feeding them bad meat again. The Yollin stood, his two thick legs marking him as lower-class, but that only mattered were he a member of civilized society. In space, he was more mobile than his four-legged counterparts, a couple of which served as members of his crew.

He didn't mind lording it over them, but they were outcasts, just like him, just like the entire crew.

P'tok had his mandibles surgically reduced to fit within an environmental suit. He wore a custom one at all times, because he never knew when they'd find new prey.

He hoped the next ship would wait to appear until after he carved a chunk out of the carapaces of his environmental chief and head cook. His face took on a grim air as he left his station. The bridge crew breathed a sigh of relief and returned to work.

The *War Axe*

"What do you think?" Terry asked. Char hung her head and nodded.

Lieutenant Kurtz nodded, too. "I say we make the offer."

Terry chewed on his lip. This wasn't something to be taken lightly. It was a one-way trip to a different place that Kurtz had yet to understand. He hadn't changed into Pricolici form. He wasn't afraid of losing control, but the colonels were.

Terry, Marcie, and Char were standing a little stiffly when Edwin, Samantha, and Nick entered. All four unenhanced members of the tac teams had the modified genetic makeup to create Pricolici. From Char and Terry, through Cory, when her blood mixed with the Vampire Akio's created the conditions that changed those injured and repaired most often.

"You know why you're here?" Terry started.

"We get some special skills?" Edwin asked with a grin.

"Something like that." Terry hung his head for a moment before looking up and making eye contact with each of the three warriors. "You have the markers that the Pod Doc can use to turn each of you into Pricolici, Werewolves that walk upright. It's very rare. Very. I know of three others, well, four--" He looked at Kurtz. "--in the known universe."

"Damn straight!" Edwin exclaimed as he started to strip. Samantha turned around.

"Hang on," Terry cautioned. "This comes with a lifetime of change. This isn't for picking up girls after doing tricks at the local bar. Pricolici are bad-ass. But it makes you a target, too. You'll have to control the rage that comes with the change. If you don't, then you may lose yourself to the beast and won't be able to change back."

Char stepped forward. "This isn't a game." She glared at Edwin until he stopped smiling. "If you do it, you do it as volunteers with the understanding that you will be differ-ent. Your circle of friends will shrink, and our demands on you will grow. No normal human will be able to match your strength, but they will be able to blow you away. Take a round to the head? You die. Your body gets blown apart and your nanos can't put you back together? You die. As Were, we'll always be first into the breach. You've all been there. You know there will be pain. You know that you are going to get hurt, badly and often."

Marcie nodded. "And you'll get to see into the Etheric dimension, which will make you a valuable resource for rooting out others from the UnknownWorld, for finding your enemies before they find you."

Edwin looked at the others. "What are we waiting for?"

Terry turned and spoke over his shoulder. "Ted, spin it up. We have three volunteers to become Pricolici. That'll give us an entire fire team of them. Stand the fuck by, people. Your world is about to get rocked."

CHAPTER FIFTEEN

Terry stood in the back of the classroom. It had been seven days straight of classes on alien cultures throughout Federation space. Terry was fascinated by the variety and listened intently. He asked for extra material from Smedley and read late into the night, every night.

He also paid attention to the physics of space, as he expected to be involved in epic space battles. He spent time in the shuttle pods and was greatly relieved by their similarity to the pods that he'd gotten used to on Earth. He acclimated quickly, as he knew the others would.

"I dub thee, drop ships," Terry had told the pods as they were racked in their launch positions at the side of the hangar bay. Terry was one of the most well-read people from Earth. He devoured books and loved anything by Andre Norton, Asimov, or Heinlein. The Mobile Infantry from Heinlein's Starship Troopers used drop ships.

Terry thought it a fitting tribute. He had saluted the pods. It would have looked odd had anyone seen him, but it had been only him and Dokken.

With each new class on the cultures and wars that had been fought, Terry gained confidence that the universe preferred not to fight and when they did, they weren't very good at it. He preferred not to fight, but if someone forced his hand, he made his enemies pay, making them suffer on the way to their demise.

Char squeezed Terry's hand and his attention snapped back to the class.

"Where were you?" she asked, knowing her husband all too well. With the overload of information regarding alien cultures and space warfare, his imagination was running rampant as he wargamed all the scenarios for which he would have to train the FDG. Train them to be a viable business entity known as the Direct Action Branch of the Bad Company.

"Drop ships, my lover. It's like the Marine Corps all over again, training for amphibious landings against a determined enemy, but they don't have a chance because we're us, we're the baddest of the bad-asses. That's what I see from everything I'm hearing," Terry whispered.

He was not being arrogant. He didn't do that with Char. TH was being honest. He thought back to the day they attacked a den of Weretigers. Outnumbered five to one, Terry's tactical teams never lost a single warrior. He and his people had been hurt, but not killed. Only a few Weretigers escaped.

"That's what I'm hearing, too, but do you see the cities on some of these planets? Cory, Felicity, and I are going shopping, so you better make lots of money at this," she teased.

Terry started laughing until warriors in the back row of chairs turned to look at him. He quieted and apologized.

He had no doubt they'd make money. Terry was good at what he did.

The chairman of the Federation's private conflict solution enterprise.

Delivering the right amount of violence at the right time and place, for the right price.

"Those fucking classes will be the end of me," Valerie complained. Robin rolled her eyes, which started to lose focus as if she was falling asleep. Her mouth hung slack as if she was ready to pass out. "Stop it!"

Garcia looked like he had something to say. Valerie stared him down, but he waited. "Well?"

"Bloodsport is confirmed. I've got that big dude in round one," Garcia said.

"That's nice. Bloodsport. The death matches without the death part? Leave us out," Valerie declared.

"But you'll square off against the Weres and Colonel Walton himself." Garcia showed his teeth. He loved watching Valerie fight. She was a demon.

He'd never seen the colonel fight, but had heard the stories from Kurtz about Terry soundly beating Forsaken in hand-to-hand combat. Of his epic leap into a pack of Weretigers.

He had learned from the Marines, from Kung Fu masters in China, and from Akio. And he had the experience of surviving countless battles.

"The colonel?" Valerie asked with a raised eyebrow. A hint of a smile formed. "I'm in."

In between classes, they started the matches, using the rec room to hold five contests at a time. The rings were smaller than what they were used to, which gave an edge to the brawlers, but Terry didn't care.

A warrior could try to choose their battlefield, but it wasn't always possible. Terry had no sympathy.

He personally attended Garcia's match. The sergeant nodded to Terry Henry before bowing to his opponent, the man who was the same size as Edwin before his conversion into a Pricolici.

Edwin was somewhat larger now, but he was away from the fights, training with Char and the other Pricolici. Learning to change and control their new bodies. Terry steered clear of the new Were, until they were better trained and he could incorporate them back into the FDG as a tactical team.

He would have to see them in action so he could best deploy them.

When the colonel returned his attention to the ring, the referee, one of the warriors, raised his hand and called, "Fight!"

Garcia immediately stalked sideways while the big man jumped back and forth, trying to trap the sergeant in a corner.

"You know what I love about a good fight?" Garcia said with a hint of smile that was clearly meant to taunt his opponent. "The taste of it the next day. When you wake up and taste the blood lingering. Better than a cup of coffee."

The big man's face scrunched up in confusion, then he let out a roar and charged.

Terry cringed as, even though Garcia had dodged out of the way, the big man snatched him by the edge of his uniform and flung him around. Both moved like a whirlwind, and then the big man landed on top of Garcia.

Damn, maybe the sergeant wasn't the great fighter he had been built up as.

A laugh from Garcia made Terry wonder if it was too early to judge, however. Even more so when the sergeant had scissor-kicked his opponent, one leg to the side and one to sweep out his legs, and then he was on top.

"WOO!" Garcia shouted, then brought down two solid blows before the big man blocked and countered.

To his credit, the man was damn strong. He broke Garcia's hold and was lifting him up to slam him into the wall before the other could react.

Strong, just not as tactical as Garcia. At the last minute, Garcia broke the grip by slamming down with his forearms, then had maneuvered around his opponent and locked him in an armbar that sent him face-first into the wall.

The big man stumbled back, fresh blood on the wall and his face, and growled.

"You toying with me, boy?" he shouted. "Fuck that!"

Again, the big man charged, but someone from the crowd said, "Stop trying to charge him!"

It actually worked, giving TH hope that this big man could be trained to fight the likes of Garcia. However, he clearly wasn't ready quite yet, or Garcia really was just that good. Wide haymakers came Garcia's way, and the more experienced fighter demonstrated his ability to bob and weave before finally coming back with a right cross that he immediately followed with a hook from the same hand.

The effect was that the big man went staggering backward, losing his balance. When Garcia came in with a side-kick to the guy's gut, it did the job and the referee shouted, "That's enough."

He gave a look to TH, who nodded.

"Winner," the referee announced, "you're moving on to the next match. Loser, sorry, but remedial training."

The big man stood, looking like he was about to curse out the referee, but instead turned and stomped out of there. Good. He had control. Not a lost cause at all.

The first UnknownWorld bout pitted Joseph against Timmons. The two had sparred for well over a hundred years, but it had been a while since their last match.

They bowed to each other and smiled as friends did. Joseph stripped out of his ship suit and wore shorts and a t-shirt. No one had seen him so casual before, but he was living his new life as a daywalking Vampire, never again to be Forsaken.

Petricia and Yanmei paired off in the next ring. Joseph had wanted to watch his bride, but he had his own fight to worry about.

Timmons was usually the aggressor, but he changed his tactics to be defensive and that threw Joseph for a loop.

They circled, feinting and jabbing, neither landing a kick or a blow.

"Come on, pasty!" someone yelled at Joseph.

"You'd be pasty too, if your skin hadn't seen the sun in four centuries!" he yelled back good-naturedly. Timmons dove forward in an uncharacteristic move to wrap up Joseph's legs. Joseph sidestepped and launched a pile driver into the back of Timmons's head. The Werewolf planted face-first into the padded deck and lay there, out cold.

"One and done!" the referee shouted, raising Joseph's hand.

"Pasty's got skills," the same warrior called out. Joseph nodded to the man and walked from the ring without having broken a sweat. In the next ring over, Petricia and Yanmei were both sporting split lips. Yanmei complained that she never fought in human form.

"Change then, I don't care," Petricia said with bravado she usually reserved for her wrestling matches with her husband.

Yanmei didn't wait. She changed into a Weretiger and shrugged out of her clothes. The tiger reared back and screamed, and all other bouts stopped to watch.

Petricia danced and ducked, refusing to provide a stationary target for the creature. Weretigers were fast, but not as fast as Vampires, Petricia hoped.

The Weretiger lunged. Petricia stepped forward at vampiric speed and punched. Yanmei turned her head enough to deflect most of the blow. She twisted and lashed Petricia with a paw full of seven-inch claws. Petricia cried out in pain, the slashes across her arm and chest starting to rain blood onto the mat.

The Vampire stepped back, but Yanmei pounced. Unbalanced with three hundred pounds of great cat on her, Petricia fell over backwards, flailing to throw the Weretiger from her. Yanmei rode the Vampire to the ground, striking her head twice in less than the blink of an eye.

The Weretiger bared her fangs and screamed in Petricia's face. Pinned, Petricia thought she was going to die.

"STOP!" Joseph yelled, charging in and hitting Yanmei with a body block. The Weretiger rolled aside and came to her feet with a snarl. Joseph held his hands out in surrender. Yanmei screamed one last time before changing into human form. Naked, she rushed to Petricia's side, joining Joseph who was already there.

Aaron appeared with a towel to wrap around his wife, while Cory asked them all to step aside.

She laid her hands on the worst of the wounds. The familiar blue glow began, signaling the passage of nanocytes from Cory to the injured Vampire. Both hands glowed and Petricia visibly relaxed as the pain disappeared.

A few more seconds, and Cory pulled her hands away. She stood unsteadily. Ramses appeared and helped her to a seat.

Valerie watched it all with great interest. "Terry Henry jumped into the middle of a pack of those?" she whispered to Garcia.

"Yup, and those were mostly males twice Yanmei's size," Garcia replied, pursing his lips.

"Damn." Valerie bit her lip, a crazy idea seeping into her mind. "I can't wait to get a turn with the tiger. What do you bet I can get it by the tail and swing it around?"

"If you do that, you'll be fighting two Weretigers, the colonel, and Major Char all at the same time. It wouldn't end well for you."

"Another challenge, huh, Garcia? You're going to owe me your soul before we get off this ship."

Yol Space

The Singlaxian Grandeur glided gracefully behind a moon and slipped into a tight orbit, where the ship powered down most systems and made believe that it was a hole in the expanse of space.

P'tok sat in the captain's chair, glancing at the displays lining the walls surrounding the bridge's consoles. Passive systems provided his only source of information.

A rough-looking Yollin entered the bridge. Scorch marks across his carapace suggested he'd recently been in a firefight. He smelled of ozone and melted steel.

"What was the haul?" P'tok asked softly, as if the sound of his voice would carry outside the hull and give away their position.

"They had nothing, my captain, except weapons and the desire to fight. That's why we blew the ship."

"So they might have had something, but you weren't willing to fight for it? That's what I hear from your excuses."

"My captain. We would have died and gained nothing except the information on our ship sent to the entirety of the pan and loop galaxies. We would have been pariahs for the remainder of our days. This way, we can continue to ply the routes. Those expecting that ship will believe it was an engine failure. Because of my actions, we live to fight another day," the soldier said boldly.

"You cut and ran. Get out of my sight while I think on what to do with you." The captain's mandible stubs worked back and forth in his agitation. He spun his chair around and looked back at the screens, watching for a telltale moving spot of light indicating a ship was searching.

P'tok believed their prey had transmitted a distress signal. Regardless of blowing the ship, he believed the Singlaxian Grandeur had been compromised.

One big score and I'll buy a new ship, replace the crew, and find a new route with new, choice targets. Yes. That's what I'll do. One big score, he thought.

CHAPTER SIXTEEN

The *War Axe*

Terry and Char stood on the bridge watching the enormity of space on the screens designed to look like clear windows. They gave a nearly three-hundred-and-sixty-degree view from the bridge that stood above the aft section of the ship. Like an island, it commanded a view of the warship before and beneath it. Weapons bristled from its hull, side to side and front to rear.

The variety of weapons represented the latest and greatest that the Federation had to offer. Just like the gate drive. Few ships were big enough or important enough to have the wormhole technology.

Captain San Marino embraced the magnitude of his position, and Terry knew a professional when he saw one. Micky looked at the ship like Terry looked at the FDG. A capability versus a problem to be solved.

"A problem not yet defined, nestled within a strategic direction guided by a moral compass," Terry said in a low voice.

Char couldn't read his thoughts, but she knew him as well as he knew himself. "The frailty of mankind is its strength. Those seeking a legacy beyond their mortal selves will carry us to the future."

Terry searched his mind and couldn't find where that quote had come from. "I haven't read that, but it sounds like something I would like."

"It's not written down. Maybe I should write a book." Char smiled and her purple eyes sparkled.

"There are those who say they want to write a book, and then there are those who actually do," Terry prompted.

"I know you've been keeping a journal, and Cory, too. I missed having a computer, because if I write, that's where I'd do it. What was the point of complaining? But now, there's no excuse. You are on, Terry Henry Walton!" Char stuck out her hand, which TH took and shook firmly.

They turned their heads at the same time and caught the captain watching them with a strange expression. Terry looked at the man and asked, "Are you married?"

Char shook her head.

"I call my wife the Battle Axe," Micky replied.

"And you say that out loud?" Terry asked in surprise.

"You know her as the *War Axe*."

"A demanding mistress, indeed," Terry exclaimed when he caught on. "I shall protect your fair partner with my life!"

Terry bowed.

"As will I!" the man at the helm declared.

"I won't," the Yollin grumbled.

"Heathen!" someone cried from the group near the engineering displays.

"Okay, maybe I will," the Yollin continued to grumble.

Micky grinned. "I've been on other ships where the embarked force was at odds with the crew from day one. But not you guys, and that is refreshing."

"One team, one fight, right?" Terry said.

Char gazed at the screens, turning as she looked from one to the next, getting a view of the entire solar system that they would soon leave behind.

"When are we gating away?" she asked.

"Jumping into new space requires the crew to be ready. Say the word that your people will be manning their stations, fully capable of entering strange and possibly hostile space."

"Hostile space? Aren't we jumping to Yol?"

"The gate links between here and very specific coordinates. But, those coordinates are the weak spots in space's fabric. I'm afraid in known space, they are well defined, as in, everyone knows where they are. There will usually be a ship of one sort or another that is waiting near the target coordinates in every system we go to. Mostly merchants wanting to sell us something. We once were accosted by a ship full of dancing girls and guys. It took us a week to shake them off because the night crew kept letting them dock with us."

"You weren't the night crew," Char accused.

The captain smirked.

"I was, but we were unanimous in our decision."

"My people can get a little wound up. If you bring dancing dandies on board, I will have to cancel training until we can get them off."

The captain chortled, and the bridge crew started to laugh.

"Let me rephrase that…" Terry stammered. Char put a hand on his arm and shook her head. *Too late.*

"Give us another week," Terry told the captain. "We have our Bloodsport contest going on. We'll finish that in a couple days. Give the people a chance to heal while we gear up and conduct a little more practice with the railguns and plasma rifles. You have some nice toys on here that we are more than happy to take off your hands."

"Have you seen the mechs?" Micky asked.

"I'm sorry… Mechs?" Terry started to grin. He had always loved tanks. He would have had an Abrams after the WWDE if Char hadn't talked him out of it by using sound reasoning.

"One-person mech suits. Armor for the discerning ground pounder. We don't have a great number of them, but we can make more. We have the production capability, but we'll need more raw materials. We should be able to get that when we get to Onyx Station."

"Where are the suits?"

"Forward armory."

"There's a forward armory?" TH asked unnecessarily.

"I'll ask Smedley to show you the way."

"I live to serve," the EI said over the bridge speakers.

"Or Dokken could show us," Char offered.

"Dokken will be available shortly as Jenelope is currently chasing him from the mess deck."

"Works for me. If you'll excuse us, Skipper, we've got places to go and mechs to see. We'll speed up the timeline in getting our people ready to staff the drop ships. I think it's about time we gate to a new galaxy."

"I think so, too, TH," Micky replied.

"This looks like a maintenance bay. No wonder we missed it." Terry and Char looked at the large roll-up door that Dokken was pointing to.

They were waiting for the enhanced senior staff of the FDG to arrive. Terry wanted the opinions of his most trusted people--Kim, Kae, Marcie, Auburn, Cory, and Ramses.

Terry and Char leaned heavily on their family. They relied on the pack too, but Weres wouldn't be operating the mechs. They'd probably be driven by enhanced humans, as all the FDG was becoming. Most of the warriors had completed a third trip to the Pod Doc and were stronger and faster.

They would also live much longer lives.

As Terry and Char's family members arrived, Terry accessed the panel and the door opened. His jaw dropped as he saw a workshop with a number of armored suits. They were completely enclosed.

He hadn't realized that he was expecting an exoskeleton type setup. These were sleek, about half again as tall as him, a rocket launcher mounted on the shoulder and various connectors for other weapons that were neatly stacked in a wall rack. Plasma rifles, railguns, sonic disruptors. Similar to the standard weapons, but much bigger.

"I love this universe!" Terry was first to hurry in,

followed closely by Kae and Marcie. Auburn walked to the assembly line to look at the construction process, but he was thinking about recovery and repair. He'd seen what Terry Henry Walton did to his equipment.

Ramses smiled as he looked at the suits while Cordelia frowned. "What's wrong?" he asked.

"What kind of battles are you expecting to fight where such weapons are needed?" she replied.

"Battles like every other. We wouldn't go into combat with the intent to lose. Weapons like these can help us to intimidate an enemy into talking as opposed to fighting. You know us. That's always our goal," Ramses explained.

She knew it was true. "But the other people don't know that. The aliens don't know that. We're going to take the drop ships and invade alien planets. They are going to fight back when they see weapons like these. And how am I supposed to heal anyone when they're buttoned up in one of those?"

Cory pointed an accusing finger at the mech suits.

"That's why we bring you along, my dear Cordelia," Terry said, ignoring the suits and giving one hundred percent of his attention to his daughter. "You help us to see what we can't. Of course we want to talk first, so we will probably need to keep the mechs hidden. If the shooting starts, we'll do everything in our power to finish it as quickly as possible."

She nodded because she trusted her father. Her real worry was that Ramses would don the armor and disappear into battle. She kept that to herself.

Kaeden opened one of the suits and climbed in. With Smedley's help, he powered it up. The rear access sealed and the suit looked seamless. He took a few tentative steps, making the others dodge out of the way. He worked the arms for a few seconds then faced a second suit. Kae used his arms to pick it up, almost fell over, adjusted, and lifted the suit to the ceiling. He moved to the weapons rack and delicately removed one of the plasma rifles.

He aimed it, and that was when the others ducked and ran for cover.

"STOP!" Terry Henry bellowed. Kae froze, then slowly lifted the weapon.

"Damn, Dad. You didn't have to yell so loud," Kae said, using the suit's external amplifiers. "You should see the information you get on the displays. It's like I'm not wearing a helmet at all, but I can see three hundred and sixty degrees without looking over my shoulder. There's a map of what's in front of me right over here, and then there's a full inventory of weapons and load out. You won't believe what this thing can do."

They picked themselves up and dusted themselves off as Kae put the rifle back in its rack, parked the suit, and climbed out.

"We can do some serious damage with one of those," Kae said, bubbling with joy.

"Or six of those," Marcie said, joining him in his adoration of the mechs.

"What about our normal folks? Can they operate those things?" Terry asked as he peeked inside the suit.

"With ease," Kae replied firmly. "It was no effort at all to drive that beast."

Terry looked at Char. "You know you want to," she said.

He did.

TH climbed in. The suit sealed behind him without Terry having to do anything. He tested the arms and legs as Kae had done. It was as easy as walking. Picking up the other suit only required balance. If he fell over, he assumed it would be easy to get up since the suit mirrored his motions.

He asked the others to clear the way and he walked into the corridor, took a left, and then a right on his way to the hangar bay.

Kae and Marcie each climbed in a suit of their own and followed the colonel. Ramses and Kimber each took a suit.

"What the hell," Char said. She climbed in and tested the suit by getting into a couple yoga positions.

"Is that how you're going to use the suit?" Cory asked. Char heard her clearly.

"Just seeing how it all works," Char explained as she studied her displays. Dots were overlaid on a map. Each dot was clearly labeled with who was inside the suit. She expected the EI had something to do with individual identification based on the chips in their heads. "It looks like the others are in the hangar bay."

Char walked slowly with Cory as they made the short walk to the hangar bay through the over-sized corridors that were unique to that section of the ship.

Garcia moved easily through the rounds until there were only four left to battle it out for the top spot from the initial group. They'd started out as unenhanced, but thanks to the Pod Doc, they were all stronger and faster.

It presented a unique challenge.

Garcia flexed and stretched as he prepared for a bout against a wiry woman. He was remiss in that he'd discounted her and hadn't watch her dispatch her opponents.

When the bell rang, he moved forward a step, then two as part of a feint. She stood straight up as if surprised he would try such a tactic. He turned his feint into an attack, which she blocked and counterpunched, connecting the heel of her hand to his mouth and nose. Garcia stumbled backward while defending with a flurry of punches and kicks to hold her at bay while his senses came back to him.

When he shook off the cobwebs, he set himself anew and moved sideways, offering openings for her to attack.

She did and he dodged, but not quickly enough. He grunted when her foot impacted his exposed chest. Garcia wondered if she'd been enhanced more than the rest of them.

He watched and waited, successfully blocking a number of attacks. She had a tell, giving away her next move, which came so fast that he could barely see it coming, let alone stop it, but it left her right side vulnerable.

Garcia opened himself and started his counterattack before he saw her move. His boot impacted her ribs hard enough to double her over, and he followed with a driving jab to her temple, which finished her. No one cheered as the blood dripped down Garcia's face, as he bent in half with his hands on his knees, gasping for air, happy that the match was over.

He almost fell over as he took a knee next to the woman. Her eyes rolled around as he helped her to a sitting position. She tried to focus on him, but couldn't. "Nice one," she muttered.

Garcia looked around, but couldn't find Cordelia or any of the senior leadership. But the Vampires were there. Valerie nodded to him in recognition of his victory as she approached and took her position in the ring. There were four left from the UnknownWorld. Yanmei squared off against Robin while Joseph faced Valerie.

"Let's watch that one first, before I kick your ass into next week."

"It wouldn't be the first time my ass has been kicked thusly, my dear," Joseph said with a slight bow of his head. Valerie looked at him oddly.

"You almost sound like you enjoy it," Valerie replied. When he shrugged, she chuckled. "Then you're gonna love me."

Yanmei didn't bother with ceremony. She entered the ring as a Weretiger, yellow eyes narrowed and watching the Vampire closely as she padded in a wide circle. Her muscles rippled beneath her orange and black pelt.

Robin sized up her opponent. Valerie had wanted to fight the Weretiger. She was disappointed that Robin had drawn that bout.

The Vampire chose the tactics that would end the bout the quickest. She ran straight at the Weretiger, hitting Yanmei with a shoulder block, lifting up and throwing her into the air.

Robin caught Yanmei by the neck, twisted and slammed her head-first into the mat. The Vampire dropped to a knee and side-kicked the Weretiger out of the ring. Yanmei crashed into the first row of bystanders, wheezing from the broken ribs. The referee called the match, victory to Robin.

The Weretiger's claws and fangs were free of Vampire blood. Yanmei had not landed a single blow. Robin nodded to Yanmei and walked out of the ring.

Joseph frowned. "I had hoped for a longer reprieve from my ass-kicking," he said softly. "No matter. Master referee, on your mark."

Joseph stepped aside and bowed deeply to his opponent. He returned to his stance, knees flexed and arms out, hands ready as the Marine martial arts had taught him. He'd learned more as he had been taught by Akio, as had the entire pack, but he didn't want to show his hand too early. Petricia, fully healed, cheered him on.

Valerie didn't pull any punches. She moved close and squared off, and they whaled on each other at vampiric speed.

Since all of those watching were enhanced, they were able to follow the action, but would have been helpless had they been in the ring. They would have only seen the first blow coming. After that, stars and darkness.

Apropos, considering they were in space.

Joseph dipped slightly. Valerie didn't go for it, she hesitated, just long enough for Joseph to miss a block. She jabbed, tagging him on the chin, followed by an uppercut that he blocked, but found himself outplayed when Valerie's roundhouse landed on his temple, staggering him.

She sent a second, harder swing his way. He went down in a heap, then immediately rolled to his back, but his hands were up and he was laughing.

"I surrender to you, dear lady. You are my better. Have

mercy on my old soul." Valerie smirked, looked at the referee who declared her the winner, and walked from the ring.

She'd already fought and beaten Robin. In her mind, there was only one fight left.

Colonel Terry Henry Walton.

CHAPTER SEVENTEEN

The mechs danced and cavorted on the hangar deck until TH asked Smedley to open the doors and disengage the field. As soon as Cory put her hood on and grabbed onto a ring at the side of the bay, the EI sealed the bay from the rest of the ship and slid the great door open. Smedley turned the forcefield and artificial gravity off.

Terry jumped upward, executed a somersault, and planted his feet on the ceiling when he hit. The mechs had magnetic grappling as well as claws on their boots. They also had jets that resembled micro-thrusters. Terry pushed off slightly and tapped the pneumatic jets located in the back of the suit.

The colonel led the way, but the others soon followed him into space. They cruised along the outside of the hull, exploring, and practicing flying and bouncing.

"Follow me," Terry said playfully as he angled toward the aft island that contained the bridge. The six suits lined up and flew past the bridge monitors, one by one, showing off for the captain and bridge crew.

"Back inside," Terry ordered. The others maxed their jets in a race to be first onto the hangar deck. Terry let them get ahead as they tried to outdo each other. He turned and decelerated as he approached the upper frame of the entrance to the bay. The others overshot it while Terry slipped smoothly inside, maneuvering close to Cory before settling to the deck and clamping himself down.

When the others joined him, he asked Smedley to close the doors. The forcefield flickered into place and the doors slid shut.

"We need to return the suits to the forward armory where the bots can conduct a maintenance check on them. Seems they've not been driven about before," Kae told them.

When the air returned, the hatches opened and the mechs walked easily down the passages and back to their shed. They parked them where they found them, and climbed out.

Marcie was the most excited, jumping up and down with Kaeden like a little kid.

Terry's smile disappeared as he watched. "As much as I'd love to take one of these into combat, these aren't for us. Marcie, Kim, Kae, and Ramses, please select wisely. The people in these are going to be force multipliers and they are also going to be targets, taking all the incoming fire of the biggest weapon systems the enemy has. These need to be used wisely, and it can't be us. We need to be on the ground and ready to talk, should an enemy decide they've had enough of fighting a losing battle. If they decide to keep fighting, we bring in the heavies."

Kaeden was crushed. The others were disappointed,

too. But it was different. Kae had taken a liking to being the FDG's weapon specialist.

Terry pulled his son close and whispered in his ear. "I'll need someone I know well to lead the mechs, interested?"

Kae brightened. "I can't think of anything else I'd rather do to contribute to the success of the next mission."

Over the next three days, Terry ran the FDG through constant drills loading and unloading the drop ships. They trained. They studied. They worked long hours.

All the while, Valerie bided her time.

Garcia was up against the reigning hand-to-hand champion from San Francisco. But that match kept getting delayed as the colonel was unhappy with response times.

People weren't moving quickly enough or in sync. He wasn't a fan of the mob approach. The Force was broken into six landing parties, one for each pod with every warrior carrying their full combat load, weapons, rations, explosives, and other combat gear.

Terry, Marcie, Kae, and Auburn had a field day with the gear available on the *War Axe*, and ended up cutting the load in half from their initial eyes-bigger-than-their-stomachs approach. Terry and Marcie were getting too excited for combat. Auburn became the voice of reason.

"Remember what you used to say? It's best to win without fighting, or something like that."

The colonels appreciated the sanity check. "Indeed, Auburn, but look at this stuff! Plasma rifles, selectable handguns, railguns, and then this baby!" Terry patted the

Jean Dukes Special at his side. The others wondered if he slept with it as they hadn't seen him without it since Kae had given it to him.

"Loading up!" Terry declared, and they separated out the tactical teams.

Terry and Char led one. Sue and Timmons, Marcie and Kaeden, Ramses, Cory, Shonna, and Merrit, Joseph and Petricia, and Kimber, Auburn, Aaron, and Yanmei.

Valerie expected to lead one, but Terry refused because she hadn't trained or operated with the FDG before. He put her on his own pod for two reasons: He and Char always took the most difficult part of all operations and he felt that he could control the Vampire.

He knew that she was faster and stronger than he was, but wasn't sure she could be the teammate that he wanted her to be. As soon as she proved herself to him, he knew that he would put her in charge of her own tactical team, despite everyone else's objections.

She wasn't an insider like Terry and Char's pack and family.

Maybe someday. Terry was torn. If he lost the fight to her, he suspected he wouldn't be able to bring her into the fold. If he didn't fight her, he expected the same result.

He had to fight her and he had to win. In the brief periods that he allotted for sleep, he studied her fighting techniques, but he only had three bouts to watch, each lasting only a short time. Each time, she used slightly different tactics, but always she counted on her superior strength and speed to overwhelm her opponent.

He watched, studied, and planned. He put it off until he couldn't put it off any longer. TH designated a time and place for the final two bouts of the contest they'd called Bloodsport.

"I can't put this off any longer. I have to fight her," Terry told Char.

"I know," she replied simply. "And I know you're going to win. She may be as fast and strong as Akio, but she's not trained like Akio. Don't worry. Get your sleep and fight with a fresh mind."

"Two days after the fight, sooner if no one is beat up too badly, we will jump away from Earth. For some reason, I don't think we'll return. It's gnawing at the pit of my stomach and I don't know why."

"You're leaving home. As fucked up as the world's worst day ever made it, it was and will always be our home. Others have built this ship and given us a purpose. Until you've made that your own, you won't be comfortable." Char stretched luxuriously. The bed was smaller than they were used to, but Terry was okay with that.

They'd been married a long time and he had gotten used to his Werewolf wife's heat. Her body temperature was much higher than an average human's. He had gotten heat rashes when they first spent the night together, but after they shared nanocytes, it became natural to sleep next to a roaring furnace.

"What would I do without you?" Terry asked as he traced a finger down her naked body.

"Be miserable, lonely, and probably grossly misguided," she teased, as her eyes sparkled and her smile drew him to her.

"Probably. I know that I'm supposed to conserve my energy, but…"

Garcia wore only shorts, just like his opponent, Flynn, who they called the Mighty Flynn. Once TH had called him that, it stuck.

The sergeant bowed to Corporal Flynn, who dutifully and respectfully bowed back. They took their stances and Colonel Marcie Walton dropped her arm to signal the start of the bout.

They darted in and out, circled, and darted again. Kicks, punches, and leg sweeps. Nothing hit home. They danced away and started circling again. It seemed like they had taken forever to accomplish nothing except tire themselves out. Marcie signaled an end to the round, which surprised them. None of the bouts in the Bloodsport contest had gone more than one round.

"I guess this makes us special," Flynn said.

"Yeah. Don't expect another break," Garcia growled. When the colonel started round two, Garcia charged. Flynn axe-kicked him in the middle of his back, driving him to the mat. The corporal followed with a stomp, but Garcia rolled away, coming back to his feet in one smooth motion.

He stretched his back, but the bruise was there and his muscles already sore. He shook off the pain and crouched low as he approached. Flynn was slightly taller with better reach and Garcia decided to grapple to limit his opponent's advantage.

The four Pricolici knew Garcia fairly well and taunted him mercilessly from the crowd. They hadn't been allowed to participate because they were not yet in control of their abilities. If they changed during a rage, they would kill their opponents.

That was a non-starter, so they were on ice and practiced in a closed, strictly-controlled environment. Char expected that it would take months for them to gain control over their nanocytes to work with them and not let them take over.

Garcia smirked and flicked his head at his old friends. They took physical fitness to the extreme. He was glad they weren't in the contest because he knew that he could only beat them one out of three times before their change.

A blow hammered into his eye, driving him backwards. His momentary distraction had left him open. Garcia tried to cover up, but Flynn rained the blows into every opening that Garcia gave. In a desperate move, the sergeant dove to the mat, rolled, and jumped upward into a flying round-house kick. Flynn had followed, expecting to deliver the knockout punch. He was caught by surprise and took the full force of the kick on the side of his head.

Stunned, he stayed upright, but his hands fell to his side. Garcia landed and rotated his hips and shoulders into an uppercut that lifted Flynn off his feet. The corporal flopped to the ground, bouncing once, before lying still. Marcie jumped into the ring to check on the Mighty Flynn.

Alive, but not kicking. Someone delivered smelling salts and that jerked him back to the present.

"Fuck me," the man mumbled.

Garcia dropped to his knees, took two deep breaths, and puked his guts out.

Marcie pointed to him. "You're the winner! Congratulations, Sergeant Garcia. I'd raise your hand but I'm not coming over there."

He waved her off. "Very funny, Colonel," he said softly, but he was smiling. He looked for Valerie and Robin. They both golf-clapped for him with a slight nod.

Terry Henry stepped into the ring and helped Garcia to his feet. "Well done, Garcia. Way to keep your wits about you even after that beating you took." He helped the man from the ring and delivered him into the arms of his fellows. He looked for a chair so he could sit down.

He had taken a beating and his nanocytes had a lot of work to do.

A bot appeared from somewhere and cleaned the ring.

Terry stepped into it and Valerie joined him. He bowed deeply. She bowed in return. Terry smiled, appreciating her efforts.

He didn't bother with feints. He had no intention of offering an opening because he knew that she could take advantage of it more quickly than he could cover up.

He started to swirl his hands as if conjuring a magic spell. He'd learned that as part of his Kung Fu training at the monastery as a way to deal with a quicker opponent.

Valerie balanced, knees slightly bent as she stalked TH. She watched his hand-swirling, timing when best to strike. She lunged forward and jabbed. Terry deflected the majority of the blow, but it still clipped his chin.

He danced away and continued his arm swirls. She came in again, slightly overextended. He grabbed her hand and pulled it to his chest as he turned. Valerie punched him in the back, breaking two ribs and driving one of them through Terry's kidney.

TH felt the pain, but had already committed. He wrenched her fingers sideways, pulling with both hands until every finger was broken. He dropped with the second punch to his back, but kicked out, catching Valerie in the knee.

He rolled to his back, sending a lightning bolt of pain through his body. Terry kicked again, driving the Vampire's kneecap upward. She staggered away.

The colonel stood up as fast as he could, which was still slow. Valerie hopped on one leg, trying to block with her bad hand while punching with her good hand. Terry caught the broken fingers and twisted, pulling himself toward her.

He rotated at the waist to put more power behind the elbow strike that caught her in the mouth. Her teeth cut the hell out of his elbow, but her head snapped back.

She wasn't finished. She pounded his ribs with rapid blows. Although they would have felled a normal person, they weren't with as much power as her previous strikes. Valerie was on her heels.

Terry was almost ready to go down. Stars were shooting before his eyes. He dodged backward, spun, and kicked through Valerie's bad knee. The leg buckled and she went down. Terry staggered away.

She was furious. Her hand and knee were ruined, but she was fully conscious. The Vampire urged her nanocytes to work more quickly. But she couldn't stand. Marcie stepped in and declared the match over.

Terry had won, but there was no cheering. He was badly injured, blowing pink frothy bubbles with each wheezing breath. He stumbled to Valerie. She was furious.

She was in better condition than him. Her injuries were only superficial while his were life-threatening.

But she had lost.

The colonel offered a hand. "We have a date with the Pod Doc," he told her.

"What, that's considered a win?" she asked. "I wasn't dead yet."

"Here it's a win, yes. Those were the rules. For FDG purposes, a disabled opponent can almost be as good as a dead opponent. If we can disable them, then we can kill them at our leisure. Assuming they need to be killed, of course. All depends on the ROE, the rules of engagement. On Earth, when we fought, it was important to keep as many people alive as possible, because Earth needed to repopulate to survive. Out here? Who knows?"

Terry helped her to her feet and she hopped on one leg, wincing as her ruined leg flopped with each bounce. "Well done, Valerie. Know that I won't fight you again. There's no need. We both proved our points. Now, if you don't mind, I'd like to get to the Pod Doc."

"Stop right there!" Char insisted, motioning to someone outside the ring. "After that, you both think you're just going to walk up a flight of stairs? What the hell is wrong with you?"

Two stretchers appeared. Terry didn't feel like arguing. Although his nanocytes were performing heroically, he was feeling worse by the minute. Poisons from his destroyed kidney were flooding his body. One lung had collapsed and the second was in danger. The injuries were internal, which meant that Cory couldn't fix them.

Kim and Char took Terry's stretcher while Marcie and

Robin carried Valerie. The warriors ran ahead of the procession to clear the way.

When they arrived at the room, they found it locked with Ted inside. Char was incensed and pounded on the door while the stretcher lay in the corridor. "TED!" she screamed. "Smedley, you better open this door and fire up the Pod Doc right now. I will rip your electronic guts from this ship and launch them into space. OPEN THE FUCKING DOOR!"

It finally slid to the side. Ted stood, upset with the interruption, but became confused when he saw Terry as they hurried in and helped him into the Pod Doc.

"Is the ship under attack?" Ted asked.

Char ignored him. "No," Marcie replied. "Just us doing what we do."

"Do it somewhere else next time," Ted said matter-of-factly.

Char closed the door and jabbed a finger into Ted's face. "Fix him," she demanded.

"Just like a dog, one fixing coming right up," Ted chuckled. Char grabbed him around the neck.

"You know that I will fucking kill you," she snarled.

"I know, I know. Relax. Let me finish this so you can leave."

"Just do it," Char said as the Pod Doc started working its magic.

Garcia and Flynn showed up. They both looked gray. "While we're here, if we could get a few minutes in that thing, we'd appreciate it," Garcia said. Flynn winced as he tried to smile.

Marcie looked at the mob in the corridor. "HOODS!"

she yelled. The response was instantaneous. Even Char pulled her helmet on in one smooth motion.

"Four seconds to the last one of you," Marcie declared. "Well done, people. We gate out of here in two days. Say your good-byes to Earth and get yourselves ready. Go on now. I think we're good here."

CHAPTER EIGHTEEN

Micky looked at the stars, knowing that in moments they would change. The gate drives were active. The FDG were secure in the shuttle pods. The crew was locked down and ready.

The captain tapped his controls. "All hands, helmets on. We will activate the gate in ten seconds. Ten seconds, people. Count us down, Smedley."

The EI dutifully counted down, changing crew status from red to green when three seconds remained. Had there been someone who had not put their helmet on, Smedley would have stopped the countdown at one and contacted the crew member and anyone near that person to help them out.

It was the standard operating procedure, the SOP, for all gate travel. If the ship jumped into the middle of a meteor swarm, the ship could lose atmospheric containment instantly. Micro-meteors could be catastrophic for ships. The *War Axe* was better armored than most vessels, but they complied because it made sense to have the damage control teams standing by.

It was better to have them and not need them, than the alternative.

"Gate forming," Smedley reported.

In front of the ship, a large ring appeared. It gave Micky goosebumps, and he shivered in anticipation. The ship eased across the event horizon, which was where the majority of the gate engine energy was directed.

It had turned out that establishing the wormhole was the easy part. It took the Kurtherians a long time to figure out how to manage the travel across the event horizon in such a way that kept the ship from getting crushed. Once that was solved, it made travel throughout the universe possible, broadening the reach of the alien species. And then the humans found their way to the stars by way of Kurtherian technology.

Thanks to Bethany Anne, humanity now played a key role in universal affairs, in the ever-expanding Etheric Federation.

Terry and Char watched on the drop ship's screen as the gate appeared. Terry checked everyone quickly and they were all secured. He relaxed as the *War Axe* moved into the shimmering ring. There was a brief indescribable sensation and then the ring was gone and the star pattern was different.

The ship stopped. "Stay where you are. We have to wait

for the all clear," Terry said through the bubble of his helmet.

He heard a bang and pop. Terry switched views and saw that the hangar bay door was opening and the bay itself had not been depressurized first.

Terry had studied the SOP on gating and nowhere did it say the hangar doors would open upon arrival. They didn't need them open to launch the pods, which faced outboard from the side of the ship. They only needed the doors open to recover the pods.

"Smedley?" Terry asked.

The instant the ship arrived, the bridge ran checks and verified that systems were reactivating. The gate drives took too much power and active systems could throw off the wormhole targeting.

Everything non-essential was powered down during the establishment of a gate and the transit. All systems were immediately energized upon arrival. But there was always a lag.

A red light flashed, showing that the hangar doors were opening. The forcefield was not yet in place. Atmosphere vented explosively through the crack of the doors. Usually, the forcefield would contain it and the venting would occur at one time, reducing the stress on the door seals.

"Why is the hangar door opening?" Micky demanded.

"External control, sir. Smedley is trying to stop the process, but it appears that he's locked out," K'thrall reported.

"Sir, a ship is approaching," the helm reported.

"A Yollin raider, I suspect," Micky said more calmly than he felt. He tapped his controls. "Colonel Walton. We are under attack. A Yollin raider will be landing on the hangar bay momentarily. If you would be so kind as to repel the boarders, I would be eternally grateful."

<hr>

P'tok saw the wormhole establish. "Stand by!" he broadcast throughout the ship. As the great warship came through, he saw the vulnerable bay doors. "Activate the override."

He had purchased the program from a Londil less than a year earlier and had already successfully used it a number of times. It would be obsolete sometime soon, but that was not this day.

The Yollin watched the puff of air as it escaped when the doors popped open. The doors continued to slide back, showing a massive hangar bay that looked empty. "Our lucky day. Take us in," he ordered and the pilot accelerated forward, touching the main engine to gain momentum while using thrusters to align the Singlaxian Grandeur with the opening.

The ship darted forward and closed rapidly on the *War Axe*. "Now is the time for redemption, my brothers. Brace for impact." P'tok yelled his war cry as his ship flew into the bay and due to the expert abilities of his pilot, landed with a slight thump.

"Gold and glory!" P'tok shouted in their tradition. If they pulled off this raid, then maybe he could retire.

Terry heard the captain's plea. With a snarl, he activated his pod's comm link with the other pods. "You heard the man. Maintain unit integrity, four by two, limit your attacks to sonic blasts within the hangar bay. Joseph and Kimber, your teams may be able to get an angle where the open door is behind your targets. If so, turn your railguns loose. No friendly fire incidents. Go, go, go!"

The six pods popped open and the warriors rushed out. Some hesitated as the carapaced creatures emerged from the enemy raider. They wore a massive bubble over their heads because of their mandibles. They wore a separate suit over their bodies, but the carapaces showed through. The first warriors opened up with the sonic disruptors. Two warriors fell when the disruptors had no effect on the Yollin, and they returned fire with slug throwers.

"Joseph!" Terry yelled when he saw how ineffective the nonlethal fire was. Many of the crew carried swords that they'd won in combat or acquired over the years. Terry carried a Mameluke made with Damascus steel from a bygone era. Akio had killed a Forsaken who carried it and given it to Joseph initially, who traded Terry for a shorter cavalry sword.

The Mameluke was a Marine's weapon. Once a Marine, always a Marine. Terry never carried a sword into combat when he'd served in the Corps, but it was a new world and he had bested many foes with the blade. He waved it in front of himself as he ran toward the nearest Yollin, zigzagging on his approach.

The alien held his ground as he fired at the approaching

human. His slugs bounced harmlessly off the inside hangar walls. Terry stayed on his feet, taking small and unpredictable steps. If he leapt at the Yollin, he'd give him a target.

Terry dodged right at the last instant, ducked and spun. He hit the Yollin with every bit of strength in his body. The Mameluke cut halfway through the creature's body before it stuck. Terry kicked the alien backwards, but the sword didn't pull free. With his foot on the creature's chest, he pulled his Jean Dukes and thumbed the lever to three, blowing the creature into the deck.

The sword came free, and Terry looked for his next target. It was chaos. His people were mixed up with the aliens. He couldn't see past their ship to see what was happening on the other side. A Yollin popped out of the ship in front of him and then disappeared in a spray of guts and red mist as a railgun round tore him apart.

Terry looked for the shooter and found a warrior standing next to Petricia, as if protecting her. She looked out of place, being unarmed. He shook his head as Joseph waded into a melee with a large Yollin using his rifle like a club to block Joseph's sword attacks.

All of a sudden, Joseph decided he'd had enough and sped up. Time seemed to stop as he slashed three times, shredding the alien.

A whirling dervish broke into the middle of a Yollin band. Valerie wielded her European-style sword while Robin moved at her side with two short blades, the women fighting as a single entity. A round from a Yollin's slugthrower slammed into Robin. The Vampire slapped a hand against her chest to hold her suit closed as she continued to swing with deadly efficiency.

Valerie didn't give them a target they could hit. The railguns ripped the Yollin apart and the tide of battle was swinging. A great blast sent a shockwave through the hangar bay and most of the FDG went down. Terry swayed on his feet but stayed upright. The pack and long-term enhanced were still in the fight.

"They fight like demons," K'thrall said.

"Fearless," Micky San Marino said as he watched the battle unfold on the hangar deck. The warriors from the Force de Guerre were engaging the Yollin in hand-to-hand combat, using their weapons as clubs while the aliens fired into the groupings, seemingly indifferent if they hit their own or not.

An alien jumped from the ship and rolled a device in the path of the warriors. He stepped back. Only K'thrall knew that he was smiling. "Run!" he yelled, but it was too late. The device exploded and the shockwave slapped the weaker humans down.

But they'd been enhanced and weren't killed. They fell and struggled mightily to get back to their feet. Terry and his inner circle waded into the fray. Lights flashed off the blades as they whirled in deadly arcs. The Yollin were consolidating their forces to punch through and get into the ship.

"If they get to the hatch, they can cause a lot of grief.

Structure, respond with your damage control gear and prepare to repel boarders," Micky said flatly.

"Yes, sir," Commander Lagunov replied over the comm channel before closing the link.

"Sensors!" the captain yelled, ripping his gaze from the battle on the hangar deck. "Tell me there is no one else out there, please. We are here with our asses hanging out."

The bridge crew had already been engaged. Only the captain and their Yollin crewmate had been distracted by the battle.

"We are alone. Getting pinged from a ship well within the heliosphere, but they are two days away," the systems station reported.

"Very well," Micky said, blowing out a breath as he returned to watching the battle.

Terry ran around the front of the Yollin ship, saw the open hatch, and seized the opportunity. He bolted into the ship with Char close behind him.

When the two Vampires saw Terry and Char head in, they followed.

Terry blasted the first Yollin he saw, using his Jean Dukes Special. Then he hesitated. *Smedley, how does a Yollin surrender?*

>>**They grasp their mandibles and duck their heads,** << the EI replied.

Thank God, Terry said. The alien he had just hacked down had not done that. He started running again, looking for a stairway as he assumed the bridge was up and not down.

Toward the rear of the ship, he found what he was looking for and raced up the stairs three at a time. Char followed, both of her Glocks in her hands, her fingers on the triggers as Terry had told her not to do a million times. He told her to exercise trigger discipline and a million times, she ignored him.

She even shot him one time to demonstrate her trigger control. Dokken didn't care, he ran up the stairs behind Char. Valerie and Robin were behind him, trying to get past and be first into the fight.

Terry tore through the hatch and headed toward the nose of the ship. He guessed the bridge was up one more level, but the stairs had ended. He wondered what kind of madman designed a ship without direct access between decks.

Two Yollin appeared. The first one grabbed his mandibles and started to bow. Terry relaxed for an instant as the second alien aimed a rifle over the back of the first. Terry dodged and Char fired. Twelve rounds later, both Yollin lie dead in the corridor.

Terry started running again, peeking in hatches as he passed. Char checked too, as she passed, but Valerie and Robin started to fall behind as they opened the doors to get a better look inside. Terry and Char disappeared through a doorway and pounded their way up the stairs.

"Get us the fuck out of here!" P'tok yelled, furious at the inevitable failure of his attack. He had every intention of leaving the other raiders behind.

"Powering the drive system now," the pilot stated.

The ship answered the call and the systems across the board showed nominal. The doors were still open and it didn't matter whether the forcefield was in place or not. It was made for ships to fly through it. Its sole purpose was to keep the atmosphere in.

The bridge crew called out their readiness checklist.

P'tok was livid. He'd been engrossed with the battle and hadn't prepared the egress strategy.

"Where did all those humans come from?" he roared.

Valerie saw the edge of a mandible appear from behind the door. With a quick stroke, she hacked the mandible off, and the alien screamed in pain. She stepped in and swung, but had a bad angle and her blade bounced off the Yollin's carapace. She followed with a thrust that impaled the alien.

She yelled defiantly as she charged, ramming the alien against a bank of equipment. Sparks flew from the tip of her blade when it cut into the panel. She yanked backward, pulling the sword out.

The Yollin slowly toppled. Valerie quickly searched the space. They were alone, but the equipment was starting to hum.

CHAPTER NINETEEN

Terry vaulted up the steps and found the door to the bridge. Terry was surprised to find it open. How could they not know that their ship had been boarded?

Terry hesitated for a step then jumped through and dodged to the side, running into a Yollin at a workstation against the back wall of the bridge. Terry fired at point-blank range. The pistol was still set on three and it bucked slightly, but the Yollin was blown apart, and his station arced and sparked as the projectile burrowed deep into it. Terry dodged past the dead alien, now that he had the undivided attention of the other three on the bridge, including the one that looked to have almost no mandibles sitting in the center seat on a raised platform.

Char dodged to the other side and aimed her pistols, ready to fire.

The aliens were torn. Dokken barked furiously.

The one that Terry thought was the captain looked to be in rage. He shook with his anger. The others had hands poised over their work stations.

"Time to call off the attack," Terry told the Yollin. "My name is Terry Henry Walton, and you're on my ship."

The Yollin relaxed, and his eyes darted to the screen showing the battle. A mech had appeared and was rounding up the Yollins who had survived the human onslaught. The shimmer of the forcefield returned and the hangar doors started to close.

"Punch it!" the captain called out. A knife flew past his head and embedded in the neck of the pilot. His hands went limp and he fell face-first into his console before sliding to the floor.

Valerie stood in the hatch, her sword covered in alien blood.

The second Yollin attempted to use the momentary distraction for his own heroics, but his station wasn't designed to fly the ship and he had to mash one button too many. He died when Terry hammered him with a projectile on the number one setting. Even the weakest was enough to penetrate the alien's carapace. The Yollin wasn't thrown back, he simply jerked and slumped, leaving the workstation intact.

"It looks like we want a setting of one for close quarters combat," Terry told the captain. "Do you know what a sheriff is?"

The Yollin didn't answer.

"Well, there's a new one in town, and you've pissed him off. I'd love to just blow your head off, but I think we'll need to talk with you about some things. Your life is mine and your continued survival depends on your cooperation. I expect you're a pirate or some fucking ass monkey shit like that, which tells me that you're not so keen on giving your life for your cause. Make no mistake. I will kill you, and I'll kill you ugly."

P'tok didn't deal with humans very often, but the ones standing on his bridge had a different look to them. He wasn't afraid, but knew that he should have been.

"Fuck you. And you too, buddy. Fuck all y'all!" Kae yelled using the mech's external speakers.

As soon as they had received the colonel's call, he ran for the forward armory. Marcie and the rest of the team from their drop ship covered him. He powered up the system and made it to the battle in time to break the spirit of the rallying Yollin. After the detonation of their incapacitation bomb, they thought they had the upper hand.

Kae squashed that quickly when he appeared wearing the battle armor, a mech that no Yollin could stand up to. Their weapons fired subsonic ammunition in order to limit hull penetration.

Old fashioned slug-throwers, not even as advanced as Char's Glocks.

In the end, Kae rounded up ten prisoners. Twenty-two Yollin lay dead along with two warriors who were injured so badly that their nanocytes couldn't save them. Thirty-seven warriors were injured.

The forcefield was restored and the doors slowly closed. As atmosphere returned, those who could drew back their hoods and experienced the smell of propellant, of a ship's engine, of the dead and dying.

Kae sobered as the bodies were stacked. Yollin hands were zip-tied behind their backs.

Marcie waved for Kae to stay where he was. She gathered the pack, along with Kim and Ramses, to board the enemy ship. Cory stayed behind to help the worst of the injured.

Marcie was wary, but found it easy to follow the path the colonel had taken. There was a trail of dead bodies and alien blood.

"I am Captain P'tok," the Yollin announced as he removed his helmet and grasped his mandible stubs in surrender.

"Why would you attack a warship like this?" Terry asked.

"We have a saying in Yol. Who dares, wins," the captain replied.

"We have the same saying. I have to say that your name means asshole in Klingon. I won't be able to say it with a straight face, but that is neither here nor there for you. Come on, douchebag. It's time we introduce you to your new home."

The Yollin's translator chip didn't interpret a number of the human's words, but he understood enough.

He bowed his head in defeat. There would be no new ship and no need for a new crew.

Terry nodded to Char, who pulled out a zip-tie and bound the Yollin's hands behind his body. He looked a bit like a satanic effigy.

Who was now Terry and Char's prisoner. "Looks like

we have ourselves an infiltrator ship. Hey, dickface," Terry called. "What's this console do and can we fix it?"

"It is a general sensor console. And to answer your second question, I don't know, can you?"

"I'm starting to like you. Do you know what that means?" Terry asked. The Yollin didn't answer. "I'll kill you last."

Valerie and Robin stood aside as Captain P'tok was escorted from his own ship. Terry stopped and turned to Valerie. "Thanks for stopping the pilot."

"Any time, TH," she answered, before entering the bridge to retrieve her knife. She'd almost forgotten it in the excitement.

I'd really like to bite this captain, Dokken told Terry.

I'm with you there, buddy. He's quite a dick, but we have to protect him now that he's in our custody. That's kind of a human thing, Terry replied.

For the record, I think it's stupid, Dokken said. *I so want to bite you.*

Dokken growled his dismay at the Yollin.

"Smedley, I need you to make sure that can't happen again. How in the hell did they implement a system override of our hangar bay doors?"

Micky was angry. His ship was in one piece and they had acquired a second ship, which should have been cause for celebration, but the FDG had lost people. Micky had failed his embarked force by letting intruders on board.

The *War Axe* should have blasted that ship from space,

but they never had the chance. The ship would always be vulnerable, but they could lock out the doors to prevent them from being remotely opened. And the fire control systems could be on standby, returned to full power more quickly.

The ideas raced through Micky's mind.

"So much to do," he mumbled. He tapped his control panel. "Terry Henry Walton, are you there?" he asked over the ship-wide intercom.

There was no answer.

"Smedley, where's the colonel and the other senior leaders of the FDG?"

"Sir, they are aboard the Yollin raider."

"Alive and well? How many did we lose?"

"They are alive and well. It appears that they have eleven prisoners, ten in the bay and the colonel and his entourage are currently escorting one from the ship."

"Get me all the information you can on that ship, and find out how they opened that door!" Micky ordered before getting up and hurrying from the bridge. "I'll be in the hangar bay," he yelled over his shoulder.

Terry was working his way from person to person as they lay in rows of the injured, telling each one something to buoy their spirits as they started the healing process. Most would be recovered before the day was done. Others would need time in the Pod Doc. Those who had been shot had gotten help from Cory and were on the fast track to health.

Cory was lying at the end of the row, with Ramses hovering over her. There had been more injured than she could deal with and she was dangerously depleted.

Two warriors had already been taken to the Pod Doc. Char had told Smedley that the door had best be open and Ted ready to receive the injured. Smedley played nice on Ted's behalf. Char didn't care as long as the warriors were taken care of as soon as they arrived.

The captain appeared and joined Terry Henry in thanking each of the injured for the role they played in securing the *War Axe*.

Terry stopped and stood. He turned to the captain. "If we hadn't been aboard, what would you have done?" Terry asked.

"We would have lost a great deal before flooding the passageways with firefighting foam, and that still might not have stopped them."

"This great ship and you would not have been able to stop a platoon of pirates?"

"Not once they got on board. We have already removed that vulnerability and will notify General Reynolds and Nathan Lowell regarding the incident. We have been ordered to Onyx Station immediately," Micky explained.

"What are we waiting for?" Terry asked.

"It takes a bit for the gate drives to recharge and I want to give your people time to heal. We'll leave in a day."

Terry continued down the line of injured, stopping with Cory and putting a hand on her cheek. She was sleeping with her head in Ramses's lap.

"I'm glad you found each other," Terry told his son-in-law. "Your only job is to be here when she wakes up."

"I know," Ramses replied. "There's no other place I'd rather be."

Terry gripped the man's shoulder. He waved the rest of his closest people to him. The Were, the Vampires, and his family.

"Welcome to the other side of the galaxy, where there are plenty of fuckers who need to be killed. You've seen them. You've seen what they can do. They hurt us, but now you know. We can kick their fucking asses. Kae and Marcie, take a good look at our load out. We were useless against them except with swords. Look at body armor and weapons.

"We got a lot of our people hurt because we had to get too close to the enemy. Auburn and Kimber, get with the skipper's engineers and dig out any weaponry and technology our new infiltration ship carries. Hang on."

Terry walked to where the Yollin prisoners were on their knees. "Hey, ass monkey, what's the name of my new ship?"

"The Singlaxian Grandeur," he replied after clicking his disdain.

"The Grandeur. I'm good with that." He looked at his inner circle. "Find its secrets, including the technology that allowed it to access our hangar bay. Gather all the weapons and add them to our own. We can use a good low-penetration gun, just in case we're boarding spaceships. And find that fucking bomb they used. I want some of those in our inventory. Joseph, Petricia, Valerie, and Robin, put together a security detail to move these goofy bastards to the brig. You do have a brig, don't you?" Terry asked Captain San Marino.

"We do, but it'll be kind of cramped. It was never intended to house enemy prisoners of war."

"I don't give a goat fuck if they are miserable. Secure them. I expect once we're on Onyx, we'll be able to turn them over to the intelligence branch of the Bad Company. You four go with them. Don't put up with any bullshit from them. Get them into the cells and lock them away.

"We've arrived in a new part of the universe and we're already blooded. Space is a dangerous place, but we are not someone to be tangled with. Let the reputation of the FDG and the Bad Company's Direct Action Branch start here. The first battle streamer will fly proudly on our flag."

"We don't have a flag," Char said, already knowing how TH would answer.

"Not yet."

Terry gave the aliens the finger before he walked back toward the ship with Kaeden and Marcie in tow. Char watched them go. "I'll make the funeral arrangements," she said softly.

He heard her, as he always did. He looked over his shoulder. "Thank you," he said just as softly.

The captain watched the purple-eyed Werewolf. "We'll set it for tomorrow. Before we gate, we can launch their bodies into the event horizon where their atoms will be scattered across the universe."

"Make it so," Char replied.

Terry disappeared into the raider's ship. Injured warriors were being moved from the hangar bay. Joseph and the pack were pushing the Yollin prisoners toward the hatch to the interior of the ship and the nearby brig.

The battle was over.

The first battle was won, not because of superior weapons, but because of the tenacity of the human spirit. A month earlier, Yollins would have been considered monsters.

Now? The enemy was no longer big and scary. They died just as readily as any other living creature, as long as you knew where to hit them.

The hangar door was open, but the forcefield was in place. The bodies of the two fallen warriors and the Yollin raiders had been loaded into a forward launch tube. The Force de Guerre stood in formation, looking at the swirling pool that was the gate. They'd already said their good-byes.

"Hand, salute!" Terry ordered. All the warriors saluted. "Fire."

The bodies were launched from the tube toward the edge of the gate. They disappeared in a flash.

"Ready, Two!" The unit dropped their salutes. Even Valerie and Robin had saluted.

Terry liked what he saw from the new additions.

"Company, when I give the command to fall out, you will fall out and fall in your drop ships. Secure yourselves. We jump in one minute. FALL OUT!"

The warriors scrambled as they ran for their ships. Terry lingered as he looked at the beauty of the gate. The hangar bay was clear. He gave a thumbs up to where he knew the camera was that projected the image from the hangar bay to the bridge.

Terry ran to his pod, the rear deck closing as he made it inside. He assumed his seat and activated the comm link to the other pods. "Hoods," he said. "Smedley?"

"Three-point-nine seconds. A new record, Colonel."

"Thanks, General. Give the captain the green light for us."

"He already has it. Jumping in three, two, one…"

Terry's body tingled with the sensation. Char looked to be more comfortable, smiling at him, but he saw the goosebumps on her arms. "You're trying to out-tough me?" he accused her.

"I've been out-toughing you for the past one hundred and thirty years," she stated. Terry started to laugh as he watched the screen. The hangar doors remained closed and he breathed a sigh of relief. The unit wasn't fully recovered from the previous day's jump.

The ship systems came back to life, one by one. The ship-wide broadcast crackled. "All normal. We are on an inbound vector to Onyx Station and will arrive in two hours. Colonel Walton to the bridge, please. All hands, stand down from emergency procedures."

Terry spoke to the other pods. "Prepare for movement from the *War Axe* to Onyx Station. Once there, we'll receive our orders."

The drop ship ramps opened and the warriors pulled their hoods back. Most ran for their quarters, thinking back to liberty in San Francisco. It seemed like forever ago.

It had only been a few weeks.

· · ·

Docking Bay 17. Deck 25. Onyx Station, Paladin System

Nathan Lowell stood in the docking bay and waited. Ecaterina was there as well as Christina. She didn't want to come, but he wanted her to meet the newcomers, Bethany Anne's handpicked group that would represent Bad Company interests when direct action was called for.

Nathan needed a private conflict solution enterprise sooner rather than later.

The *War Axe* was too large to fit in the docking bay, but the shuttle pods were more than welcome, with room for all six and plenty more. Even the Grandeur could fit, but Nathan preferred to send a team to assist with the technical intelligence in addition to ensuring that the thing wasn't rigged to blow if anyone tried to fly it. It was parked a few kilometers from the station, just in case.

"The pods are on their way," Nathan said unnecessarily as the lights picked up the inbound ships. The pods slowed as they entered through the forcefield, the EI communicating with the station's landing control to bring them in for a landing, side by side, in a tight formation. The rear ramps dropped and Terry Henry Walton and Charumati were the first ones off.

Colonel Marcie Walton barked commands and all the rest formed up, nearly eighty souls standing at attention. The line of Weres at the back stood loosely.

"Pricolici?" Ecaterina asked.

"An issue with renegade nanos and a runaway Pod Doc," Nathan explained. "There is a Werewolf on board that is some kind of genius. I look forward to talking with him, maybe ship him over to R2D2 to join Team BMW. We can use some fresh minds."

Terry marched to Nathan Lowell with Char walking purposefully by his side. Her purple eyes were clear even at some distance. Cory's blue eyes glowed behind the formation.

"What an odd bunch," Ecaterina continued. "Weretigers, Vampires, Werewolves, glowing eyes. I'm surprised they don't have a Werebear with them."

"They did, but he chose to stay behind," Nathan replied before greeting their guests. Terry saluted and Nathan laughed. Christina snorted.

"You must be the famous Terry Henry Walton," Nathan said as he offered his hand. First Terry shook it, then Char.

"Not sure about all that," Terry replied. "We were in the galaxy for five seconds and a pack of Yollin raiders gives us a bloody nose. I have to admit that I'm a bit embarrassed by that."

"Micky said you saved his ship, that's worth a bloody nose, and you picked up some door-cracking software for us. The captain of the Grandeur? Just an added bonus. I look forward to taking him off your hands. He and I are going to have a little chat."

Terry smiled. "I think I'm going to like it here. What's the plan of the day, sir?"

"Nathan, please. I have my private conference room ready for us with some fresh food and other delicacies from the sector. You might as well start getting a taste of what's before you. I've tasked some people to show your folks around. Would you like anyone to join us?"

"Maybe twenty? Too many?" Terry asked.

"How about six?"

Terry pursed his lips briefly and then nodded. "Marcie, Kae, Kim, Cory, Timmons, and Joseph, with us."

Petricia looked crushed.

"His partner?" Nathan asked.

"They are very close," Terry admitted.

"Tell her to come, too."

Terry waved and gave the thumbs up. Petricia hurried to Joseph's side and took his hand.

"If you'll follow me." Nathan walked away. Ecaterina watched with mild interest before hurrying to catch her husband. Christina glared at Char. The Werewolf shook her head, wondering what the issue was.

Christina bared a fang.

"Fuck you too, bitch," Char said under her breath. Christina slashed with a claw, but Char ducked, spun, and back-kicked. Christina easily dodged Char's best attack.

"ENOUGH!" Nathan roared, storming back to stand between his daughter and Char. "These are good people, on our side. This isn't a fight you want to pick. Go and take those two shopping."

Nathan pointed to Valerie and Robin. Christina looked upset.

"I don't care if they're Vampires. Show them a good time and if you get arrested, I'm not coming to help you."

"No one has the balls to arrest me, or is tough enough."

"Of course, dear. If you hurt someone because you picked a fight, I'll lock you up with the Yollin prisoners. Do not try my patience, Christina Bethany Anne Lowell!"

"Ooh," Char whispered. "The full name treatment."

"That never worked out well for me when I was growing up. That's why I prefer TH."

Char nodded in understanding. Christina huffed and stormed away. Valerie cocked her head slightly and rolled her eyes. Terry gave her the thumbs up.

It'll be great, he mouthed. She gave him the finger.

"While we're on a roll, Nathan," Terry said.

"Do you have kids?" Nathan asked. Of course he knew. Terry wondered what kind of test he was being given.

Terry pointed to the group with them. "My tribe."

Nathan looked from one face to the next. "I'm going to have to hear the story about why your eyes glow blue all the time. I've never heard of such a thing before. And you." Nathan tipped his chin toward Joseph. "You are much older than these young pups."

"I am," Joseph admitted without giving more. Nathan waited for a few seconds, then turned and headed toward the elevator.

***

"What the hell is this all about?" Robin demanded. Valerie raised one eyebrow, unhappy with being left out of the powwow with Nathan Lowell.

"I'm under orders to show you a good time. It's like double secret probation, all because that purple-eyed freak glared at me," Christina complained.

"Char? She's a pussycat," Valerie said with a chuckle. Aaron and Yanmei were standing next to them.

"Almost exactly that, except completely different," Aaron said, before joining another group as they walked toward a door leading from the docking bay.

"What's up his ass?" Christina asked.

"He's a Weretiger and you're not," Valerie said. She had no idea, but was already tiring of the young-looking Pricolici. "Where can we get a drink around here?"

Christina looked around quickly. "There's a seedy place called Wash It Down that I've heard is the best on the station. But aren't you Vampires and you can't get drunk?"

"That's right, but we can still enjoy the burn on the way down, if you know what I mean!" Valerie exclaimed with a grin. "Lead on, young one."

"I'm not that young," Christina said defensively.

"Like fuck. We can argue about that when we get to Wash It Down. You have money, don't you?"

"A little," Christina replied, not sure she liked where the conversation was going.

"We just got here and don't have any. So your treat and we thank you."

Christina started to rethink trying to pick a fight with Char. Then again, she was going to a bar with a couple randy Vampires looking for trouble. Maybe a good time was to be had.

Her mood improved significantly.

Terry took small amounts from each dish as he wasn't sure what he would like. Char piled a mound of what looked like raw meat on her plate.

His lip curled as he looked away.

"Still can't handle watching Werewolves eat, Terry Henry?" Nathan asked.

"Not so much. My friends call me TH, by the way," Terry said. Nathan nodded.

He held the chair so Ecaterina could sit down and then sat next. Char sat, followed by the others. Terry was the last to sit down after asking if anyone wanted anything else.

He ate sparingly as he wanted to focus his full attention on Nathan Lowell, President of the Bad Company, Pricolici, and personal and long-term friend of Empress Bethany Anne.

"General Reynolds sends his regrets that he couldn't make it for your arrival."

Terry waited. He had only questions, but wouldn't ask them until Nathan filled in some of the blanks in Terry and Char's future.

"I have to admit that we executed a little subterfuge when you first boarded the *War Axe*."

"How so?" Terry asked, eyes narrowed at the revelation.

"We took some of the nanocytes from everyone in your group and had them analyzed."

Terry leaned back and crossed his arms in a defensive posture. He felt like he had been attacked, and he didn't even know there'd been a fight.

"It's nothing nefarious. We always look to improve. We also need to know everyone's particulars in case something happens so we can put you back together. Do you know what we found?"

Terry shook his head while Char leaned against him, keeping one hand on his shoulder.

"We found that you two have created a hybrid nanocyte, impervious to the usual programming changes.

You passed those on to your daughter--" Nathan nodded to Cory. "--who passed on certain attributes to everyone she's healed. It really is fascinating. Because you two got together, you and all your people are better."

"Tell us something we don't know," Terry quipped.

"We can't replicate it," Nathan admitted.

Terry leaned forward, resting his elbows on the table. "Nanocytes. They exist because of programming. You can't download it and then copy it a billion times?"

Nathan laughed. "No. Your nanocytes have adopted their own language. The chip and other things done on the *War Axe* are with nanocytes that are working in conjunction with yours. We aren't able to enhance you further as your nanos would fight off the new ones. I'm not sure that's a bad thing."

Terry and Char shrugged. "You made me wait two years before we created the super nanos, you big bully," Char quipped.

"You were with this fabulous creature for two years before, well, before that?" Nathan was incredulous.

Char nodded.

"She was a fucking Werewolf! I didn't know what to expect," Terry replied defensively.

"I'm still a Werewolf," Char said coldly as she twirled her silver streak of hair. Cory brushed her hair back, exposing her Werewolf ears.

"Dammit, Nathan!" Terry exclaimed. "I'm here five minutes and you've put me on couch city. You can buy me a beer. Don't tell me there's no beer in this galaxy."

"There is beer. That is a true universal. Every culture has figured out how to take a grain and brew a fermented drink from it. Every culture also has its own form of Swedish meatballs, but that's something completely different. Yes, I'll buy you a beer, TH."

"We're square then. Down to business, Nathan. What do you need from us? What do you want from me?"

"I've formed the Bad Company, a commercial enterprise that trades goods throughout the Federation, although we mostly operate along the frontier. The units, and this information is not to leave this room, through the access they have by virtue of buying and selling, collects intelligence for me on behalf of the Federation.

"We have units scattered across a thousand light years. This is a vast expanse of space that we're dealing with. Besides the manufacture and trade operations that we run, I need a Direct Action Branch, which you've already been briefed on. There are an infinite number of jobs out there where one belligerent faces off against another. It upsets the balance in entire regions. They have money and we're willing to take it to help them settle their lovers' spats. There are far more conflicts than we can address, so we can pick and choose. I need you to help me evaluate the potential missions and then when we pick one, execute with the most and least amount of violence necessary to accomplish the objective."

"Mercenaries," Terry said, not judging, but he wanted it in the open.

"Absolutely. We don't hide that or the fact that we will choose only missions that we can live with. We have a stack of proposals that I'd like you to review by morning. Make your recommendations and then we'll pick one together. You'll execute it, and I'll grow richer."

"It's hard to say 'no' to that!" Terry joked and then turned serious. "What's our logistics support?"

"The *War Axe* is yours. Load it up with what you need before you leave Onyx Station. That's it for this time, but I'm going to move you closer to the frontier. Your permanent base for operations will be in the Dren Cluster, but you'll always have a link to my office, wherever I am hanging my hat."

"So we'll be fighting planet-side?" Terry wondered.

"Mostly. Remember, you get to pick the mission. Evaluate them carefully, because if you go, it's your ass on the line."

"I understand, Nathan." Terry turned to the others and waved one arm expansively. "We understand. I have one of these, a gift from Michael Nacht." Terry tapped the Jean Dukes Special on his hip. "What would it take to get one of these for each of my people?"

"You have only to ask. I can get the pipeline started, but it will take a while. These are very unique weapons, so you may not have them for the first five or ten missions."

"Damn!" Terry was taken aback. Having been flung into what he thought of as the distant future, he had a hard time believing there was anything that would take a long time. The Pod Doc reprogrammed people in ten minutes! "That'll have to work. What's the chain of command look like?"

"You answer directly to me," Nathan replied.

"General Reynolds?" Terry asked.

"He is associated with official Federation business. We need to limit our contact with him when we're doing work off the books, so to speak. The Bad Company's

Direct Action Branch is a private conflict resolution enterprise."

"That sounds familiar, but it tells me that we're on the same page, Nathan."

Nathan slapped his hand on the table. "So let it be written, so let it be done! I owe you a beer. If you would excuse us, Terry and I have places to go and people to see."

Terry leaned down to kiss Char, but she put her hand out. "Fucking Werewolf? Couch city is too good for you." She moistened her lips lightly using the tip of her tongue.

"Maybe we could find our quarters and then freshen up first?" Terry suggested as Char played with him.

"You have plenty of time later for that. I have an ulterior motive, TH. I want to check on my daughter. Our AI suggests that she has found the seediest bar in all of Onyx Station. We need to go help before all the furniture is broken and the floor awash with blood."

"That bad?"

"Do you think your Vampires are going to be a good influence?" Nathan asked pointedly.

"I was hoping Christina would be a good influence on them."

"We better hurry," Nathan said.

Terry could not have agreed more.

Valerie and Robin sat with their backs to the wall, leering at the men in the crowded bar. Christina watched them closely. There was no smoking allowed on the station, but smoke tendrils drifted through the air.

"You aren't going to take one of those back to your room," she said, making a face.

Valerie chuckled and gave a look to Robin that seemed to hint at an inside joke. "No, as fun as that may be."

A trio of young adventurers sauntered up to the table, carrying six bottles of beer.

"Mind if we join you?" the smoothest of the bunch asked.

"Sure," Valerie said with a mock slur as if she was drunk.

The men paired off, each selecting a target for their affection. They put the extra beer in front of the women.

"Ohhhhh... I'm sorry, but I don't drink beer," Valerie said as she took a drink from the beer she'd been nursing.

It was warm and tasted like piss water. "I'm a single malt whiskey kind of girl."

She'd never had it, but had heard Terry talking about it as well as the beer. She looked at the remains of her first beer, wholly unimpressed. Terry's stock went down in her eyes.

One of the men pointed to the beer in her hand.

"Single malt," she said slowly, enunciating clearly. The man's friends waved him away. He left in a huff, went to the bar, and frantically tried to get the bartender's attention. They watched him flail.

"We're usually smoother than this, but we've been out for a long time with no feminine company. When we saw you, we had to stop by."

"Oh really?" Robin droned.

"No shit! Fucking marauders, fighters, space junk, and we're lucky to be alive, but when you have a great team, you can get through anything."

"You fucked marauders but they fought you with their junk?" Valerie asked.

"No! Why would you say that?"

"I'm just saying what you said," Valerie replied.

"That's not what I said," the man answered.

"Hmm, maybe I need an illustration? I've always been more of a picture book kind of gal."

The man stopped his next retort as their friend placed six single malt shots on the table. Valerie and Robin took one without waiting, toasted, and drank them in a single swig.

"That's what I'm talking about!" Valerie raised Terry's stock back to where it had been before.

She reached for another shot glass. The man next to her leaned in and smiled at Robin, and suddenly had his hands reaching, groping. While Robin stared in confusion, apparently shocked this asshole would even try something, Valerie acted on instinct. At the speed of thought, she lashed out, breaking his nose and driving his head into the wall behind the booth.

The other men froze. Valerie and Robin shared an *oops* look, then each took another shot and downed it. Christina took one, not to be outdone, and threw it back.

She coughed once before smiling. "Smooth," she rasped.

The men looked at their comrade, out cold with his head embedded in the wall.

"Is there a problem, ladies?" Nathan Lowell asked as he approached the table.

"Another Tuesday night, Nathan," Valerie replied with a wink. "Why, something seem off?"

Nathan was not amused. Terry walked up behind Nathan and squeezed around him to take his place.

Christina picked up the last shot and downed it.

One of the two men that Nathan was studiously ignoring drained his beer and stood up. He looked at his friend with his head in the wall and then to Nathan.

"Why don't you bugger off, you old bastard. These women are ours." The man tried to stifle a sloppy belch, but it escaped anyway, leaving beer dribbling down his chin. He wiped it off using the back of his sleeve. He jutted his chin out.

Nathan's eyes flashed yellow as he tried to control his anger. He wouldn't let Christina start a bar-clearing brawl. "Come," he said in low and loud voice, staring down his daughter. Terry only nodded to the two Vampires.

"Fine," Valerie said, taking one of the fresh bottles of beer the men had brought over. Robin took another. Terry looked at the third. He reached down and grabbed it, trying not to laugh. He took a drink and smiled beatifically.

"That is fucked up, really fucked up. This is swill!"

"This is beer that I didn't have to make myself, which means it's a-okay in my book."

When Terry turned to follow Nathan and Christina out, the bartender was standing in the way.

"Who's going to pay for that?" he demanded, pointing at the man with his head embedded in the wall and blood running from his nose.

"You know you're not supposed to serve drunk people or allow smoking. One more word and I'll have you shut down. It would be best if you returned to your bar and forgot that we were ever here." The bartender started to reach out, but stopped as Nathan's eyes glowed yellow and he snarled, showing a pair of fangs.

"Just don't come back any time soon," the bartender said as he retreated behind the bar. Terry fought the urge to pummel the scumbag, but he was trying to set a good example for the Vampires. So he shrugged and followed Nathan out.

"I just love me some Onyx Station," Felicity drawled to Aaron and Yanmei as the three of them strolled along a decorated promenade lined with shops.

Felicity was put out that she didn't have any money to spend, but was promised they'd get their cards loaded with Federation credits within the next day or so.

"When are we leaving?" Felicity asked.

"As soon as Nathan's tech team finishes what they're doing with the Grandeur, we'll be leaving, heading for the Dren Cluster, wherever the hell that is," Aaron mumbled.

"When will his team be finished?" Felicity asked, starting to get worried.

Yanmei knew what she was getting at. "Probably the same time as you get your credits. All dressed up and nowhere to go."

"I will always have somewhere to go," Felicity promised.

"Is Ted going to leave the ship?" Aaron asked.

"I surely hope so." Felicity looked away, closed her eyes, and slowly shook her head. "I like going, but I don't like going alone."

Yanmei gave Felicity a hug. She didn't know what else to say. They knew that Ted would disappear into the new technology, never to reemerge. The Federation, despite the best efforts of those in charge, would exploit Ted's engagement.

Even though no one said it aloud, the Weretigers knew it. Terry and Char knew it. And most importantly, Felicity knew it.

* * *

Ted was in heaven. The technical team had set up an interface on the bridge and it was systematically accessing the computers and data from the Singlaxian Grandeur. Ted remained within a holo bubble, gyrating in a syncopated dance as his hands flicked in and out through the interface.

"I've never seen anything like it," one technician said to another. The older men were trusted insiders for the intelligence branch of the Bad Company. They'd followed Nathan Lowell on his journey through the universe. Always in the background, always there when needed, doing what had to be done.

Freeing Nathan to do what he had to do.

In the end, digging out the intelligence he wanted. No matter how much they gleaned, he wanted more.

Answers begged more questions. Always.

"He's going to save us a lot of time," the second technician said.

"I'll ask if he wants to join the team, but Nathan might have different ideas."

"Show him," the second man suggested.

The first technician produced a manual comm device that broadcast a secure signal. Nathan had the second device. There were no others. It was based on a million-bit encryption and had zero storage. Anything broadcast was gone the instant it was funneled through the device.

The first technician pressed the contact button. Nathan answered instantly.

<hr>

Nathan, Terry, Christina, Valerie, and Robin stopped by the promenade, the name given to the deck with the shops.

"You youngsters go on. Let us two old men go someplace quiet to sit down," Nathan said with a smirk.

Christina chuckled, waved, and headed toward the biggest crowd. Valerie and Robin followed Christina and soon disappeared.

Nathan led Terry to a lift that took them back to Nathan's private office. Once there, Nathan locked them in.

"You didn't ask a lot of questions, TH, but I'm sure you have them."

Terry rubbed his chin. "The Bad Company is already established as a shell. All I have to do is start evaluating proposals and pick one. You explained my logistics and administrative support, and it sounds good, by the way. I don't want to hassle with invoicing, but getting paid is important to make sure the Direct Action Branch is self-sustaining. I expect that you cannot funnel any more funds from the Federation into Bad Company activities. I'm sure the *War Axe* cost a pretty penny. I will do my best to pay back that cost."

Nathan nodded. "I'm sure you will. As long as you earn a one hundred percent success rate, we will never lack for quality clients. The right gig will pay for the *War Axe* all by itself."

"No shit?" Terry smiled and kicked back. Nathan got up from his desk and walked to a refrigerator that looked out of place in his plush office. He reached in and pulled out two bottles. He tore the caps off and handed the brown bottle to Terry. He kept the Pepsi for himself.

"Here's to a successful business venture." Nathan clinked Terry's bottle.

Terry sniffed the strong, dark beer and gingerly tasted it. His eyes rolled back in his head. "I accept that I have to become a businessman, but as long as this keeps flowing, I will do anything for you, Nathan. Plus, I get to shoot bad guys. That's my second favorite pastime."

Nathan didn't try to guess what was number one on Terry's list.

Something buzzed.

Nathan pulled a device from his pocket. He activated it, nodded, and placed the device in the middle of his desk. It projected a holographic image.

"Tell us what we're looking at, Jason," he told the box.

A disembodied voice responded. "It's Ted, tearing through the raider ship's computer systems. He's pulling the information and sorting it into some kind of order. I'll have to study his system more, but I'm sure it makes sense to him. We've been in this business a long time and never seen anything like it. We thought you should see it for yourself."

Terry wasn't surprised. Ted was where he belonged.

"Make sure he gets something to eat. He'll be angry when you unplug him, but he forgets to eat or drink for days if you let him go," Terry told the box.

The two technicians talked among themselves briefly. "We haven't been at it for very long, and he'll be done well before he misses a meal, but point taken. In case it runs long, we'll make sure he eats something and gets something to drink."

"Can we bring him on board the team?" the second technician asked.

"I think he'll find a new home in our research and development group," Nathan replied.

"R2D2," the first technician replied. "He'll have more fun with us, though, Nathan."

"I'm sure that you'll make every effort, but I suspect his idea of fun is doing exactly what you see him doing right now."

"True that, boss," the technician replied before cutting the feed.

"I hope you don't mind, TH," Nathan said, sounding apologetic. "I believe a person's family comes before all other things and I see that you look at Ted and the rest of them as your family. I'm asking you to split up your family, but understand that I am asking. If you say 'no,' then it's no."

"That wouldn't be fair to Ted. I've seen him like this a couple times before, around his nuclear reactor, the gravitic engines, and engineering challenges like those. He is where he belongs, doing what he loves. I can't take that away from him. His wife will be devastated, unless there's a great social life on this R2D2."

"Not so much," Nathan apologized.

"Then we'll split up the family. We will lose Ted if he learns of the offer and finds out that I said 'no.' I can't do that to him. Felicity will be the one we need to manage, but if she can shop, then we might be okay. Do you need a liaison here? I think she'll prefer staying on Onyx Station, for now anyway, but I don't want to speak for her. Is the Dren Cluster okay?"

"Okay?" Nathan said, making it sound like a question. "It's great for maintaining a military force that stays out of the limelight. It's a little off the beaten path. The only way to get there is with a ship that can gate itself."

"Military, big ships only," Terry replied.

"Exactly. We control most of those and keeping the station's coordinates secret means no uninvited guests."

"Logistics and comm in place?"

"Only the best that money can buy. You'll find a support station with over a thousand people, manufacturing, ship construction and repair, extra forces to choose from."

Terry pursed his lips, leaned forward, and looked intently at his new boss. "More forces are good. What kind of engagements do you think we'll find?" Terry asked.

"All kinds, but don't take any missions that look like protracted land wars. I think you'll want to stick with those that can be accomplished in a month or less using hit and run tactics. Win the war and move on."

"We can do that." Terry took a long drink from his beer. "Amateurs talk tactics. Professionals talk logistics. Will I be getting a regular supply of beer? And since you're showing off, Pepsi, too?"

"What would a man be if he couldn't take care of his friends?"

"So, no. We have to fly back here and pick up our own beer?"

"I've sent a couple pallets to the *War Axe* for you and we send a resupply fleet once a month. You're on the regular route, although the station is a black hole on the star maps, not literally, mind you," Nathan explained. "I have one more request. I'd like to keep the Pricolici here with me so I can train them, along with a small detachment of your FDG. We need a legitimate fighting force on this station."

Terry wasn't pleased with the final request. "The four Pricolici. That makes sense. We were doing the best we could, but they'll be better off with you and your family." Terry remained noncommittal about the detachment, but Nathan wasn't going to let go.

"And one platoon of your warriors."

"That's why the extra forces in the Dren Cluster. You knew you were going to take the FDG platoon." Terry was less than tactful. He leaned forward, hung his head, and looked at the floor.

"Yes. I'm not going to leave your ass hanging out. You'll be doing the Federation a great service. More importantly, I will owe you."

"Always nice to have an intel guy in your pocket," Terry said. Nathan wasn't a fan of the terminology based on the expression on his face. "I'll let our people know. We'll look for volunteers first. I hope we get them. Damn. I came up here for a beer, not to have the FDG gutted."

"Easy now," Nathan warned.

Terry locked eyes with his boss. "All right. We will make it work. I'll dial Jean to eleven, and we'll wreak havoc on the unwary on behalf of the unworthy."

"It'll be your job to make sure the client is worthy. I can't see you helping despots just because they offer the bigger purse," Nathan said.

"Narcissists unite!" Terry called out. He smirked and settled back into his chair. "You already know that you can count on me. Even if it was only Char and I doing the work, we'd find a way to get it done."

"You have your pack, your family, and some of the most well-trained forces in the known universe. You will be just fine, Terry Henry Walton. Get your people ready. You leave for the Dren Cluster tomorrow."

Terry drained his beer and handed Nathan the empty bottle. He drained his Pepsi and chucked both bottles in the recycler.

"One more thing, TH."

Terry froze in place and sighed. He wondered what other bomb Nathan was going to deliver.

"I think I have a new recruit for you."

Terry didn't bother to ask. Nathan would tell him in his good time.

CHAPTER TWENTY-TWO

Christina looked at her parents from under a troubled brow. "I miss my friends," she started, having difficulty continuing.

Nathan and Ecaterina waited patiently for her to continue.

"There is nothing more important to me than family, but I need to move on, try something new. I've heard the stories of Terry Henry Walton's exploits. What if I could learn leadership like that? His people love him, and he loves them. He orders them into battle, leading the charge, and then welcomes them home." Christina looked determined as she stood proudly. "I want to join the Direct Action Branch."

"I suspected," Nathan replied.

"I didn't," Ecaterina said softly, looking at her husband. "Where they're going, you may not come back. I don't know if I like that."

"Mothers throughout history have felt the same as their

children went off to war. It is my responsibility that we don't send TH into an unwinnable fight."

"I need you to give me a chance. I need me to give me a chance," Christina whispered.

"You better catch the shuttle to the *War Axe*. It's leaving soon," Nathan told her.

"I'll help you pack, dear," Ecaterina offered.

Christina looked at a backpack on the chair. "I have everything I want."

Ecaterina gripped Nathan's hand tightly as she searched for the right words. Christina hugged them both and walked out without looking back.

"Good-bye," Ecaterina said to the closed door, before turning to her husband. "You make sure TH takes care of my daughter without her knowing it!"

"He knows."

Nathan was two steps ahead, as always.

The *War Axe*

"I'm going to miss them," Sue said, crying. She'd worked with Felicity starting in New Boulder one hundred and thirty years earlier. They'd spent more time together than most married couples.

Felicity was having a hard time making her feet move. Tears streamed down her face. Ted looked uncomfortable. He couldn't wait to leave. He wasn't bothered with what he was leaving behind. His whole focus was on what was ahead.

"Dammit," Terry said, blinking rapidly. Char was doing

the same thing, trying not to cry. With Ted's departure, she was down to five total Werewolves in her pack.

Felicity laughed softly. She waved the purchase card she'd been given. Ecaterina had loaded it up for her. The two had hit it off. Maybe at Nathan's request because he was always two steps ahead of everyone else, but if he had gone to that extent, then Terry appreciated the effort.

She turned and entered the shuttle. Ted looked relieved and waved awkwardly as he climbed in behind her. Char shook her head. "Fucking Ted."

"He can't wait," Terry added.

Kurtz saluted as he waved the others aboard. A full platoon, without their weapons or armor. They'd get outfitted with equipment from the station. Once the last was aboard, the door closed and the shuttle lifted into the air. It rotated and headed through the forcefield into space.

The great doors started to slide shut.

"Sergeant Garcia, dismiss the platoon," Terry ordered.

"This is the hand we're dealt to tame the galaxy," he said.

"Bring it in!" he called and the warriors who had been dismissed, and were heading for the stairs, ran back to form a semi-circle around the colonel. The inner circle fell in beside the warriors.

"Look around you. This is the hand we've been dealt. Our job is to fight other people's battles and we'll do it for damn good money. That makes us mercenaries, but we get to pick the side we're on. Right over might!

"Fifty of us to take on the whole fucking galaxy. You know what, people? The galaxy is going to learn what it's like to be afraid. On the wrong side? Live in fear. They can bend over and kiss their own asses good-bye! We will compromise none of our ideals. Honor. Courage. Commitment. In all things, we will have our integrity. Think about it and get ready. Tomorrow, we go to war."

Marcie screamed her war cry. Kaeden and Kimber were next, followed by the cacophony from the platoon. Terry barked back at them.

"Dismissed!" he yelled over the cries and cheers.

The Dren Cluster

The *War Axe* materialized through the gate closer to the space station than he thought practical, but there it was. Big as life filling most of the view through the hangar bay access.

>>Colonel Walton, if you would report to the captain's conference room, we've received a significant amount of data for your eyes only.<<

On our way, Smedley, Terry replied, refusing to cut Char out of any of the Bad Company's business.

"We're needed in the captain's briefing room."

Char shrugged and took Terry's hand. Dokken appeared. "Where the hell have you been?"

You didn't even miss me, did you, Dokken accused.

"You're right. I didn't. And I feel appropriately bad about that, if it's any consolation."

It's not.

"Where have you been?"

I almost caught him, sneaking out of the captain's quarters, but he eluded me with a dastardly maneuver.

Terry looked at Dokken's face. A scratch trailed from

the top of his head, between his eyes, and down the side of his muzzle.

"Wenceslaus scratched you."

The cretin! Doom on him. Until next time, arch enemy, when you won't be so lucky, Dokken declared.

"Uh huh," Terry mumbled. He took off running with Char close on his heels. Dokken was left in their dust. He took off, but found they were faster than he was.

Dog speed! he called out as he pounded after the humans.

Terry and Char were waiting for him at the conference room.

My humiliation is complete, Dokken intoned. Terry held the door for him and the dog hung his head as he went inside.

Micky greeted them as they entered.

Terry furled his brow. "What's up?" he asked innocuously.

"A small mission, high risk, low reward, but needs done as a special favor for Bethany Anne."

"As with everything since we entered this galaxy, I don't see where we have a choice."

The captain held his tongue.

"Give me what you've got," Terry said.

The files appeared as a holographic image over the table. Terry used his hands to manipulate the files, perusing them until he found the meat of the packet.

"Singlaxia. A female has been entered into the Kost games, a contest of one-on-one combat to the death. Seems that the Bad Company thinks there are good sources of intelligence with the fight promoters. Fragments collected hint at a coup, one that we can infiltrate in order to sway Singlaxia to favor the Etheric Federation."

"They're hostile at the moment?" Terry asked.

"Neutral, but it's a hostile planet. Former prisoners turned military, many of them still involved in shadow operations, and the blackest black markets and darkest corners of their galaxy. We're to infiltrate, collect the intel, and then win the contest to gain credibility within the military leadership involved, as part of a permanent cover so that we'll be ready to make our move when the time comes. Let's see who the opponents would be," Nathan said, eyeing Char as the contestant, although he wasn't sure about the to-the-death part.

"Looks like, holy crap! Look at this fucking lineup. Is that one made of metal? How in the fuck do you fight aliens built like that? Son of a bitch!" Terry read further.

"Are you thinking what I'm thinking?" Char asked. Terry nodded once.

"I suspect so."

Valerie and Robin were draped over a couch as they watched the two-dimensional screen play a movie from before the WWDE. *A Connecticut Yankee in King Arthur's Court.*

Christina perched on the arm as she watched intently.

"Valerie, please report to the captain's conference room," Terry said over the intercom.

"This is amazing," Valerie said, barely hearing him. "You think Earth will ever have technology like this?"

Robin just made an "hmmmm" sound, too engrossed in the movie to fully respond.

"Ladies," Terry continued.

"Dammit, TH!" Valerie hissed, leaning forward to hear the next part of the movie. "How about a little peace?"

"Piece of what?" Terry replied.

"He heard you!" Robin whispered.

"So?" Valerie looked put out, but then thought better of it. With a sigh, she stood, forcing herself to remember that she was here to make a difference and be part of a team, not lose herself in the amazingness of this contraption.

Before she could walk out, Robin grabbed her leg, not taking her eyes off the screen. "Hurry up, because I'm not taking the time to tell you what you missed."

Valerie laughed. "I'll do my best."

She led the way into the corridor, to the steps, and climbed to the top where they found their way to the conference room.

Once inside, Valerie flopped down on the chair. Christina had followed and dropped heavily into the seat next to Valerie.

Terry thrust the digital file at her. "What do you think of that?"

She took her time reading it, not as a ploy but because she found it fascinating.

"You need a woman who can kick the shit out of that freak show. You and I both know that means me." She looked at Char knowingly.

Char wasn't too proud. She knew that she couldn't take the Vampire.

"The brief says each contestant gets a three-person

support staff. You can take Robin and a couple warriors," Terry said.

"I'm going," Christina butted in.

"No," Terry said without explanation.

"I'll go wherever the fuck I want!"

"Christina," Terry started as he leaned back to appear less aggressive. "You are a member of our family now. I'm responsible for you, just like your dad was, even when you thought he wasn't around. He was still responsible. I know you can fight, that's not in question, but can you join our family and be on the inside, help us all to do a little bit better. Valerie has this. She's going to be undercover and the mission is high risk.

"Valerie proved to me that she is the best fighter we have. This contest is going to be tough. Not that you can't handle it, but this is going to be theirs. You'll get your turn and soon, but it'll be with me and my people, and you'll do great."

"I want Garcia," Valerie said. "And the guy that rivaled him in the ring, Corporal Flynn."

Terry looked at Char. They agreed. "Done. And take the Singlaxian Grandeur. Nathan rigged it so one person can fly the thing. It's a little bigger, but what the hell. It's the only ship we've got that's not military. We'll take the Axe, gate you to another system where you can use one of the fixed gates to jump to Singlaxia. Then you're on your own, a situation that I don't think you have a problem with."

"Not at all. When do we leave?"

"In due time, Valerie. From the looks of these other files, we're going to spend very little time on Keeg, our space station in the middle of nowhere."

Terry and Char left Valerie to her study of the file. They joined the captain on the bridge. The screens showed the space between the *War Axe* and Keeg to be filled with an ion storm.

The sky filled with ghost white splashes, hazing the stars beyond. In an instant, the star field returned, unimpressed by the solar wind-driven mists.

Streaks and cascades, rivers and lakes. Ghosts flashing on the star field's canvas. Erased in an instant. Forever etched in their memories.

The End of Gateway to the Universe

This isn't a cliffhanger because the missions that follow will be their own full length books. This is Book 0 for four different series.

Follow Terry and Char as they build the reputation of the Bad Company's Direct Action Branch in Craig Martelle and Michael Anderle's upcoming series, The Bad Company.

Follow Valerie's exploits in Justin Sloan, PT Hylton, and Michael Anderle's upcoming series, Valerie's Elites.

Follow the exploits of the FDG in JN Chaney, Sarah Noffke, and Michael Anderle's Ghost Squadron.

Don't stop now! Keep turning the pages as Craig, Justin, & Michael talk about their thoughts on this book and the overall project called the Age of Expansion.

THE LINE UNBROKEN

Need another Walton in your life? Stay on Earth with Sarah Jennifer! To continue reading the TKG story arc set on Earth, leave the Second Dark Age behind and enter the Age of Madness in *The Line Unbroken*.

Available now at Amazon and through Kindle Unlimited.

Thank you for reading beyond the end of the book and all the way to the author notes. You are the bomb!

If you haven't read any other Kurtherian Gambit Universe books, then welcome aboard. This is a great ride across a huge universe with twenty authors collaborating and creating.

There will be forty three books that could be considered a prequel to this one. HOLY CRAP!

How did Terry Henry Walton and Charumati get together? How did they gather such an eclectic mix of individuals who happily joined them on this journey? You'll find that in the ten-book long **Terry Henry Walton Chronicles.** Do you like Valerie? You'll find her back story in the **Reclaiming Honor Series.** The **Second Dark Ages** which details Michael's return, but of course the series that started it all and the one that needs to be read first – **The Kurtherian Gambit** which will be twenty one books long.

Millions of words of back story. If you only want to move forward, we have plenty coming in the Age of

Expansion, at least forty books over the next year spread between six authors. Pick your favorites and keep reading.

Shout out to Diane Velasquez and Dorene Johnson who helped name the EI on board the *War Axe*. We went with a USMC Medal of Honor winner – Major General Smedley Butler, Smedley for short, although Terry will call the EI "General" on occasion. Micky Cocker is one of our stalwart beta readers. She helped me best capture BA's voice before turning those sections over to Michael for his final approval. So I named the captain of the *War Axe* after her.

Never hesitate to drop us a line – we love to hear from you. The customer is always right, right? We listen and do the best we can to keep things happening in a way that doesn't throw you out of the story. It's important that we keep you engaged from the first word to the last.

That's our goal in every story that we write.

I am currently enjoying our one month of fall before winter sets in. We are laying in six months of supplies because we live one hundred fifty miles from the Arctic Circle and don't know if we might lose power for a week or a month or all winter. We have to be prepared. It's that time of year to do all the stuff.

My mailbox is out by the highway that leads to people who live farther away from civilization than we do. As the snow packs against the road during the winter, our mailbox gets lower and lower. And because of getting hit by the snow plow, our mailbox is in a steel bucket filled with concrete. I built a rack to put the bucket on, to raise the mailbox. In a couple months it'll be frozen in place, but now, it won't be too low for the carrier to deliver the mail.

Those are the kinds of things we need to do up here. I

also have to make appointments to get our Blizzak tires put on – special tires to grip ice in the extreme cold. Studs don't really work because of how freaking cold it gets up here. Soul sucking, life stealing cold. We hit -50F last winter and that is ambient, not a wind chill temp.

But that kind of weather is great for staying inside and writing. The northern lights have returned (they've always been there, but we get too much daylight in the summer to see them) because it gets dark now. We've had some great shows already this new season.

That's it – break's over, back to writing the next book. Peace, fellow humans.

Please join my Newsletter at www.craigmartelle.com– half way down the page – please, please, please sign up!), or you can follow me on Facebook since you'll get the same opportunity to pick up the books for only 99 cents on that first day they are published.

If you liked this story, you might like some of my other books. You can join my mailing list by dropping by my website **www.craigmartelle.com** or if you have any comments, shoot me a note at craig@craigmartelle.com. I am always happy to hear from people who've read my work. I try to answer every email I receive.

If you liked the story, please write a short review for me on Amazon. I greatly appreciate any kind words, even one or two sentences go a long way. The number of reviews an ebook receives greatly improves how well an ebook does on Amazon.

Amazon – www.amazon.com/author/craigmartelle
Facebook – www.facebook.com/authorcraigmartelle
My web page – www.craigmartelle.com
Twitter – www.twitter.com/rick_banik
Thank you for reading the Terry Henry Walton Chronicles!

Can you believe we've now crossed the threshold of not only the eight books in my series and ten in Craig's, but our first in the journey into space? I'm amazed. You readers have outdone yourselves! Of course, I'm a slow reader so the amount of reading you've all pulled off would take me years, most likely. I commend you!

Although, some of you might be coming into this having not read my series or Craig's, I imagine. You should go back and read them, to get an idea of all that's come before. But if you really just want space opera and want to move forward, don't worry! These characters have plenty of adventures coming, and we're going to be working hard to push out the books.

Being part of the Kurtherian Gambit Universe has been a true blessing. I've learned so much writing with these amazing authors, and even more from connecting with you amazing readers. Many of you have taken the time to share your thoughts with us on our books and we are so grateful for that, even though we may not always agree, the feedback helps us to understand how different people read and interpret our books and writing. Michael has been an amazing mentor, and the work that he has done to keep these going is mind-boggling. Chris and Lee have taken that on with the Age of Magic, and now Craig is with the Age of Expansion. I hope he knows what he's getting into!

As for my own writing, because the Kurtherian books have allowed me to go fulltime as a writer, I've been spending some time putting out books on my own as well. I hope you all get a chance to read SHADOW CORPS, which is basically space opera with some magic to it. I love writing scifi/space opera, and I love writing fantasy, so it made sense for me to try writing them together. And don't worry, there's plenty more where that came from.

But for now, I must focus on Valerie. She is the future, after all, and has some pretty exciting adventures coming her way.

If you'd like to keep up to date with my works, please follow me on Amazon and sign up for my newsletter at www.justinsloanauthor.com. I talk about my writing, share discounts, and sometimes offer freebies.

I'll keep writing if you keep reading!

First, THANK YOU for not only reading all the way through the story, but all the way past THOSE two guys to get to my Author Notes, as well.

Here we are. The story that kicks off the stories (so to speak) that go into the future. Many of you know that I like to consider myself a bit of an Indie Publishing Outlaw.

It seems I did that by jumping the proverbial gun and putting out seven books (so far) with Ell Leigh Clarke in The Ascension Myth series set in The Age of Expansion.

The reason I had a chance to do that was due to Craig being in the middle of writing three-quarters of a million words (and more) on the Terry Henry Walton Chronicles.

Now, many of you know that Justin and I put out the Reclaiming Honor series together. And then I asked Craig if he would be willing to put out a Post-Apoc set of stories with an already created character.

Which, if you are an author, is kind of a bummer. I mean, not the Post-Apoc stuff (Craig already had some amazing stories in that genre, which is why I reached out to him in the first place.) No, I'm speaking to asking him to take on an existing minor character and doing something with him.

By book 02, Terry Henry was all Craig's character. When he and I started talking about the Age of Expansion, he was past ready to be writing some more Space Opera / Military Sci-Fi…

Then I had to make "that" call. You know, the one you dread?

It goes something like this…

Text Message from Mike: Craig, I have a question to ask. Can I give you a ring?

Text Message from Craig: Sure big man, call when you can.

Ring…ring…ri…<phone is picked up.> "Hey big man, how are you?" Craig tells me.

I'm good, how are you?

<fine>

The weather?

<It's like blazing hot…40 or something, I'm out in shorts.>

Oh…That's good…good… So, about that question.

<Yes?>

I just wrote some scenes about Nathan and Ecaterina and they make this "bad company" situation and now, the fans are asking me to write another series…But I can't. I mean, I can't with all of the Bethany Anne and Michael books going on right now.

<Uh huh…>

So, I know this is a horrible request (but I'm going to do it anyway), so what do you think about you taking on those characters and moving your new Space Opera about mercenaries in The Bad Company?

<Sounds great!>

…..

…..

I'm sorry, did you say you are good with this? (I stop biting my nails.)

<Sure, I think that would be fun.>

Well, hell. I've been worried sick about sticking you with yet another group of characters to work with that aren't your own.

<No, I can see…>

From here, Craig starts dazzling me with ideas, and I know that he isn't going to be eternally pissed with me for asking him…

Yet again.

To take on a set of characters and having him use those.

So, thank you, Justin, for continuing to write Valerie and thank you, Craig, for not giving me a lot of harassment when you have every right to do so!

Ad Aeternitatem, guys.

Michael Anderle

CRAIG MARTELLE

(click to go see books on Amazon)

The Terry Henry Walton Chronicles
A Kurtherian Gambit Series

Book 1 – Nomad Found

BOOKS BY JUSTIN SLOAN

The Hidden Magic Chronicles
Shades of Light
Shades of Dark
Shades of Glory (2017)

FALLS OF REDEMPTION (Epic Fantasy Series)

For a complete list of books by Michael Anderle, please visit:

www.lmbpn.com/ma-books/

All LMBPN Audiobooks are Available at Audible.com and iTunes

To see all LMBPN audiobooks, including those written by Michael Anderle please visit: